SWEPT UP IN HIM

LATOYA GARRETT

Copyright © 2024 by Latoya Garrett

All rights reserved. No part of this book may be reproduced or used in any manner without written permission of the copyright owner except for the use of quotations in a book review. This is a work of fiction. Names, characters, places, and incidents either are the product of the author's imagination or are used fictitiously. Any resemblance to actual persons, living or dead, events, or locales is entirely coincidental.

For more information, address:

Confident Queen Publishing
confidentqueenpub@gmail.com

Confident Queen Publishing
P.O. Box 144
Franklinton, LA 70438

dedication

To the hopeful

Your blessing may come in a package that looks different than what you expected. Let God have his way.

Synopsis

After a year-long courtship, Athena Rose is looking forward to becoming her significant other's wife. On the day she anticipates him getting on bended knee, he dumps her. Disappointed and angered that she wasted her time, Athena doesn't know her ex actually made room for her forever love.

Victor Cole is going through big changes in his life. He's retiring from comedy and going through a nasty divorce. Under intense scrutiny from the media, Victor tries to remain sane through his faith and a visit to Copeland, MS, where he reconnects with Athena.

Athena and Victor both fall hard and fast, but their fresh relationship is not without problems. Will their love be able to withstand Victor's celebrity status and a vindictive ex?

Ch. 1

Athena

God, I can't stand this lady.

Marty's mama loathed my very existence. God knows I tried my best to get this woman to like me. You'd think after a full year of he and I dating she'd thaw out a little. As far as I can tell, she was as frozen as a lone pack of chicken at the bottom of the freezer. You know—the pack that's encased in ice, and only a chisel can pry it out of the cold depths of the icebox.

"Marty, honey, don't slouch. You'll get a hump in your back," Mrs. Baldwin admonished.

Her extreme helicopter parenting should've expired umpteen years ago. For crying out loud, the man was thirty-four years old.

I mentally rolled my eyes at her before turning to Marty, who sat ramrod straight as he fidgeted with his spoon. He was acting uncharacteristically nervous today. Ever since he picked me up, he'd been overly agitated and clumsy with his words while avoiding direct eye contact.

"Are you okay?" I asked.

Mrs. Baldwin answered, "He's perfectly fine, Athens." I grinded my teeth.

My name is Athena.

Uh-theen-ah!

Ignoring her, I asked Marty again, "Are you okay? You've been a little off today."

Giving Marty a sidelong glance, I admired his quiet handsomeness. He wasn't a bam-in-your-face handsome, but he was cute and sweet. Though looking at him was like looking at his mother. Mrs. Baldwin was a pretty lady or whatever. Her constant meddling, offensive commentary, and the fact Marty looked like her was a hard pill to swallow. When she wasn't around, her presence was still felt. Sometimes I avoided looking at Marty directly because I hated to see *her* in him.

"I'm fine," Marty finally replied, eyes still avoidant.

"Marty..." Mrs. Baldwin called, and his eyes snapped to her. I growled under my breath.

See this was what grinded my gears. She held too much power over Marty. The weekly Sunday dinners he could not miss. Her doing his laundry. Telling him where to take me on our dates. Any gift he gave me had to meet her approval.

Like, why am I doing this to myself? Why am I putting u— oh, my gosh! The nervousness and avoiding eye contact plus his insistence that I wear a nice dress today...

He's going to propose.

I pushed away Mrs. Baldwin's bland potato soup. My nerves went haywire as I thought about Marty proposing. This was what I wanted, right?

Right.

But did I really want to marry Marty and have to deal with his mama for the rest of my life?

There were no other prospects that I knew of in this small town that held up to my preferences, but Marty was really sweet. He was a Christian. He loved his mama, his job at the bank, and he loved me.

I was fond of him too.

But his mama...ugh!

Shaking my head, I threw those doubts away, making the decision right then and there that I'd say yes. I'd suck it up to get the ring.

Tuning back in, I caught the tail end of Mrs. Baldwin's instructions to Marty. She was always telling him what to do. "...and remember what you have to do today," Mrs. Balwin said, looking at me with a genuine smile.

Before I knew it, I clutched my chest in shock, looking over at Marty. He jerkily nodded, croaking out, "Yes, Mother."

I'm getting married. Gretchen is going to hit the floor.

"Well, this concludes Sunday dinner. Have a good day, Athens. I wish you well," Mrs. Baldwin gleefully intoned. She abruptly pushed away from the table and left the dining room.

What a weirdo.

"Come on, Athena. Let me get you home." Marty pushed away from the table and threw down his napkin.

I looked over the table in confusion. Usually, I'd help clean up the table— another useless way I tried to get Mrs. Baldwin to like me. "What about the dishes? The food needs to be put away."

"Mother will take care of it."

Marty ushered me out of his childhood home to his car. We rode in complete silence back to my house. My mind surged with plans about wedding venues to my wedding dress to the guest list. And the wedding date...did he want a short or long engagement?

The car door slammed, and I jumped, not realizing we were sitting in my driveway. I watched Marty stalk around the car to my side.

This was the moment.

My moment.

***

"A whole year wasted, Gretch! Three hundred sixty-five days of dealing with his baldheaded mama, and he breaks up with me!" I fumed, pacing back and forth.

After Marty dumped me an hour ago, I raced to Gretchen's house.

"Sis, why are you so mad?" Gretchen asked, her hands propped under her chin.

I stopped pacing to glare at my bestie. "Seriously? Did you seriously just ask me that? I have good reason to be mad. That henpecked mama's boy played in my face for a whole year. I put up with the put-downs from his mama. I let her dictate our relationship—"

"For a ring from a guy you didn't even love. This is your fault."

Most of my anger drained away. My shoulders sank and I flopped down in the seat across from Gretchen and covered my eyes in defeat.

"You're right," I groused, peeping at her through my fingers.

Gretchen smirked. "I know. Let me do you favor like you did me when I needed to hear the truth about Otis's and I's situation. Do you want to hear the truth or hear the truth?"

I laughed at her throwing my words back at me.

"I wanna hear the truth." I uncovered my eyes so I could take my verbal lashing like a big girl.

Swiping her behemoth 'fro of curls from her forehead, Gretchen grinned triumphantly. It was like she'd been wanting to tell me about myself.

"I know I encouraged you to give Marty a chance, but I did not tell you to waste a year and a half on him. Y'all dated for six months before he committed to a relationship with you, a decision he told you his mother decided for him. Red flag number one. No, no I'm mistaken. Red flag number one is when he brought her on y'all's first date." I groaned as if in pain, and Gretchen snickered. "I really don't need to go any further with this, but friend, you allowed him and his mama to play in your face."

"Girl!" I sat up, slapping my forehead. "What was I thinking?" The reality of the situation hit me square upside my head. I groaned again, slouching down the seat in despair. "Gretch, am I in the throes of psychosis? I'm crazy and didn't even know it."

Gretchen laughed. "You are not in psychosis."

I glared and stabbed a finger at her. "I'm crazy, and you didn't tell me. Some friend you are. I'm walking around here skinning and grinning with Marty Baldwin and his tag-along mama on dates and stuff. And *you* let me! I need to re-evaluate our sisterhood."

She laughed until tears ran down her face, and my lips quirked. I cracked up laughing too.

"I needed that." I continued to giggle, wiping my face.

"Me too." Gretchen dabbed at her eyes. "But in all seriousness, take this as a lesson learned. Wait on God or else you'll be right back in this predicament. Probably not heartbroken but definitely disappointed, and you know disappointment is sometimes harder to swallow."

She was right.

I glanced around the living room. Sitting above the fireplace was a portrait of Gretchen and her husband Otis. It was a portrait of them on their wedding day. I loved looking at it because the love they had for one another was palpable. Otis's facial expression showed every ounce of devotion he held for her. My girl's expression was just as smitten. I saw forever in their faces.

I wanted that, and I verbalized my thoughts to Gretchen.

"Athena, you will get it. Stop trying to do God's job for Him. Allow God to position you for the right man. I'm glad He removed Marty from your life. Now, your husband can find you."

"Ugh, I know. But…every one of y'all is married. Mel and Talik, you and Otis, and Sherrie and Owen are matches made in Heaven. I'm not jealous or anything, but…I don't know. Waiting is hard. Honestly, something came over me when Marty told me he'd always wanted to talk to me. And then he started showering me with compliments and gifts. It felt nice to be wanted. I was addicted to that, addicted to that feeling. And I overlooked the red flags to satisfy that superficial feeling all because Marty fit the profile."

I really wasted my own time.

"I feel like a dunce."

"Stop calling yourself names. You are a beautiful, intelligent woman of God who got caught up. It happens. Do I need to remind you about my less than smart decision with you know who?"

"Please don't. You know I can't stand to even think about him." I scrunched up my nose thinking about the man who duped my bestie into an adulterous relationship. His wife outed my girl at church in front of her daddy and his entire congregation. Gretchen retreated into herself until Otis showed up in Copeland and swept her off her feet. Now, she was married with a six-month-old baby girl.

I was happy for her.

"Anyway, what I'm saying is we all make mistakes. Repent, forgive yourself, and move on."

I opened my mouth to respond, but the fine hair on my arms stood straight up.

He was here.

I turned accusing eyes on Gretchen, and she smiled guiltily.

My heart thundered in my chest as I felt him move closer. I couldn't see him, but I felt him.

I always felt him when he was around.

My legs involuntarily started crossing and uncrossing. I couldn't sit still. I was antsy like Marty was earlier. Felt like I was about to come out of my skin.

The anticipation of his presence turned me into a mess of nerves.

Always.

My traitorous body sagged in relief when he came into view beside Otis. My body betrayed me into acceptance as if him being this close to me was the fix it needed.

Like it *always* needed when he was around.

Dark chocolate skin, pearly white teeth, and drenched in the confidence of Black royalty, Victor Cole turned predatory eyes on me.

I murmured a response to whatever Otis said to me.

A slow smile eased onto Victor's handsome face. A cry from the baby monitor snapped me out of Victor's optic trap.

I discreetly let out the breath I'd been unconsciously holding.

This man had a hold over me, and I hated it. Instead of wilting like a virginal maiden in a romance book, I got mad.

I rolled my eyes at him as hard as I could.

Victor let out chuckle and walked my way.

My nails dug into the armrests.

He stopped in front of me and gave my slim legs a slow perusal. I shivered at the touch of his eyes, reducing me to mush. His eyes crawled up to my face. His smile widened mischievously.

"I see you got the toothpicks out today."

The mush turned into molten lava.

Ch. 2

Victor

Whatever feminine power Athena harnessed had me wanting to be her man. And I mean be her man in every sense of the word.

I'm talking making sure she's provided for and protected.

She had me daydreaming about lazy weekends.

Pillow talk.

Holding hands.

Letting my lips trail down the smooth lines of her neck.

On some will-you-go-with-me type behavior.

But I couldn't have her. Wanting her was wrong.

I'm a married man.

Not for long.

Legally and technically speaking, I was separated and waiting for my divorce to be finalized in the next few days.

And I should've been in the throes of grief over the loss of my marriage, but whenever Athena was around, all of my failures and frustration melted away.

She did that to me.

I didn't understand it. I tried to understand it once before until my head started to throb, but then I just accepted it as is.

My connection to her was real. Understood or not.

Athena wanted me too, but she was too stubborn to acknowledge it much less act on it.

She couldn't act on it, and neither could I.

When I met Athena last year, Shay and I had just broken up. My head was all messed up. The news of our separation hit social media and blogs, and I had to move out of the house I paid for after Shay's disrespect became too much to handle. Her social media antics, making herself a victim when she was really the villain had some fans questioning my integrity and had some business deals on shaky ground.

Even in the midst of all that, Athena mesmerized me. Her femininity, her silky-smooth walk and that rich brown skin was chef's kiss.

But I kept my distance.

My marriage of eighteen years deserved my attention so that I could mourn it's disintegration. Shay, even in her silly ways, deserved a proper dissolution to a marriage that was all good until a few years ago. Plus, I wasn't a man who started something new before handling the old. William Cole taught me to take care of my business and never leave business or people hanging.

Even if I was able to step to Athena, she was with that soft dude Marty.

Walking in my boy's house to see her sitting there looking all feminine and refreshing like a cold drink on a hot day teased me bad, and I had to force myself to stand there to keep from scooping her up and playfully brush my nose against hers in a lover's greeting.

My reaction to her was getting harder every time we were in the same vicinity.

To cover my attraction to her this time, I antagonized her.

"I see you got the toothpicks out today."

Her feline eyes narrowed into slits, and I couldn't help the chuckle that slipped out. Riling her up was too easy.

Her velvety voice flowed, "I would say something, but it'll hurt your little feelings."

Quite sure all of my teeth were showing by now.

"Victor, leave my sis alone. Always instigating," Gretchen laughingly fussed and left to check on the baby.

"I'm not bothering you, am I Athena?" I winked at her, and her eyes rolled again. "I didn't mean to bother you."

Athena said with a smirk, "As if your immature dialogue could ever bother me. Wait up Gretch." She stood and sashayed past me. Coconut and vanilla wafted up my nose as she passed. I turned to watch the hypnotic sway of her slim hips.

"Dang, Vic. Pull ya' tongue back in."

I turned to see Otis with a grin on his face, and I laughed. This fool always had something to say. "I can't help it. That's the next Mrs. Victor Cole."

Shock covered his face. "Next?"

"Yep. She don't know it yet, but once this divorce is final, I'm making my move. I tried to fight it last year when we met and every time I've been around her since."

I eased down in the chair Athena vacated. Her scent permeated the cushions.

Otis speared me with a questioning glare. "What about her dude?"

"What about him? Her dude is of no consequence to me. She's single unless she has a ring on her finger or if she tells me to step off. But she won't."

Amusement spread across Otis's face. "You a bold Negro. I respect it, but look here, Vic. Be on your grown man stuff when you step to Athena. She ain't like Shay at all. Athena belongs to God, and if you ain't trying to do right by her, you'll have to answer to God first, her mama second, Gretchen, Randall, and then me. You my bruh, for real, but I won't hesitate to come at you."

He didn't quite understand where I was coming from. Maybe he thought I was just talking. I needed to make my intentions clear. Leaning forward, I braced my elbows on my knees. "She's mine, O. That woman upstairs had my devotion at first glance. I tried to fight it. I tried. God as my witness, I fought it hard. But..." my voice dragged. I swiped a hand over my head, feeling overwhelmed by my feelings for a woman I barely knew. "I'm going to do right by her. You have my word."

Otis looked around before lowering his voice. "You sound like you in love or something."

I shrugged. "Maybe. Possibly. Man, I don't know. What I do know is I can't get her off my mind. Her presence calms the chaos in my head."

"Bruh...I...wow." Otis looked at me like I had two heads. "Okay, you ain't even got out your marriage, and you already spiritually engaged to another woman. Only you, Vic."

We busted out laughing.

"Heads up, bruh." Otis gestured towards the stairs.

I leaned closer.

"Legs texted me before we got here and said Marty broke up with Athena."

I knew he was soft. "He couldn't handle bae. All he did was get out the way for me."

Otis grinned, extending his fist. "Respect."

"Respect," I said, touching his fist with mine.

***

Back-to-back pinging woke me from a sound sleep. My bones popped as I stretched and reached for my phone on the nightstand.

Social media.

I flopped back against the pillow, phone in hand.

I already knew who it was but not what it was about this time. I contemplated turning my phone off, but I had a gut feeling I'd need my PR agent's expertise.

"Lord, give me strength," I mumbled, sounding like my grandmother. Never knew I'd get to the point I'd call on God like my O.G.

I was tired. Shay was getting all kinds of extravagant with her mudslinging. Last week, I was a serial cheater. The month before I was controlling. In private, she was begging for us to work it out, and the next she was calling me everything but a child of God.

And social media was eating it up like the thirsty blood-sucking vultures they were.

The harassment was getting out of hand from nosey reporters, Shay's followers, and the gullible people on the internet. I couldn't get any peace. That's why I left L.A. and came here to Copeland. Otis offered me a room, and I left the same day.

Ping. Ping. Ping. Ping. Ping.

I sighed, holding my phone to my chest. "This crap is never-ending. Lord, whatever it is, help me to get past this one too. I'm trying to keep my mouth shut like you told me."

Putting in my code, I tapped on the last notification.

The headline jumped out of the picture of me holding a book: *SHAY COLE SAYS ESTRANGED HUSBAND COMEDIAN VICTOR COLE CAN'T READ. SHE WRITES HIS JOKES.*

Before my anger could fester up, my phone started ringing. Marianne was calling.

"I saw it, Marianne," I answered.

Rapid-fire Spanish filled the line, and I chuckled, knowing she had to be cussing up a storm.

"Say the word, Victor, and I will unleash the beast on her," Marianne huffed.

"Nah, let her talk. I'll be vindicated." God assured me He would take care of me.

"At least let me post about your involvement with TDF. Let me do my job, so we can do damage control. She's messing with your livelihood."

Only my parents, my brother, and my team knew about my partnership with The Dyslexia Foundation.

Shay knew too.

I was diagnosed with dyslexia when I was twelve. Through hard work and believing in myself, I went from not reading at all to reading novels within a year.

I read rather well.

I might've been a little slower to finish a book than the average reader, but I finished it.

Shay was trying her best to destroy me. The girl I met in college was someone I didn't recognize. The woman I used to know and love was sweet, and compassionate, and my biggest supporter. Now, she was my mortal enemy.

The money and fame went to her head.

And as for my material, my bros in comedy knew the truth. I even wrote for many of them. I wasn't too worried about the lie floating around. I was pissed at Shay for her unrelenting attack when all I wanted to do was love her.

She broke my heart.

She was the cheater.

She asked for the divorce.

"Do what you gotta do, Marianne."

"Will do, and don't worry about this. Dreyton and Carl have rebutted the witch's claim on their IG account. People are speaking up on your behalf, Victor. Pretty soon, other people will be enlightened that Tinashay is the real villain. I can't wait for that day."

"Yeah," I said, feeling exhausted by it all.

"Hey, don't let this get you down. I know it's hard to deal with betrayal from someone who promised to love you for better or for worse. You know I know. When Raul slept with my cousin, I was devastated. When he and my cousin tried to put me out of the house and filed for sole custody of Sophia, I almost collapsed from the weight of the pain. I couldn't understand why they did what they did, and I held onto that pain until bitterness festered. I pushed people away. Then, one day I realized that their sin wasn't for me to hold onto. I was a darn good wife to Raul. I was a darn good cousin to Carmen. Was I perfect? Of course not. But I did my best. I showed up every day and I was consistent in my relationships with them both. They chose to betray me. I let the bitterness go, and I met the love of my life a year later. I'm happy and at peace."

I nodded, knowing the day would come when Shay's antics would cease. "In the words of my O.G., this too shall pass."

"Amen!" Marianne shouted. "Listen, I'm going to get right on this press release so I can shut her up. Go back to sleep, jefe. I'll call you on Monday to go over the plan for your retirement."

"Preciate ya'." I ended the call and tossed the phone somewhere on the bed.

At the age of forty, I was hanging up my microphone.

My plan was to continue to ghostwrite, do a few movies here and there, and continue investing in real estate. I partnered with Otis and his cousin Owen to open up a movie theater here in Copeland. Before, people had to drive out of town to go to the movies. Otis opened a comedy club not long after, and I followed up with Veg Out, a vegan burger restaurant.

My phone rang again just as I was dozing off.

I felt around on the covers without opening my eyes. Finally grasping it, I answered.

"Boy, didn't I tell you not to marry that girl!" my mama yelled in my ear.

I laughed. "Ma..."

Ch. 3

Venus

Me and nature started our love affair when I was ten years old.

Once upon a time, I was a girl scout. I fell in love with the outdoors when my troop leaders took me and eleven more girls on our first camping trip. Who knew that I, a very girly and budding fashionista, would enjoy roughing it and learning how to survive in case of a natural disaster or if I got lost in the woods?

Wild animals didn't bother me.

I kinda felt like Snow Black in the wild.

Anyway, after that camping trip, I was hooked. Nature hikes and yearly camping trips became a thing for me. My mama hated it, but she always acquiesced to spending a couple nights with me outdoors amongst those feral killer animals— as she would say. We created the best memories.

Inhaling deeply, I could almost smell the smores.

And the good times and great company.

Mmmm. The morning breakfast Mama used to make.

I smacked my lips, my mouth salivating at the memories.

My eyes scanned the skyline and the forestry below my perch at the top of the hill. Planting my hands on my hips, I uttered, "Lord, your craftmanship is amazing. It doesn't get any better than this."

"Tell that to my lungs," Gretchen huffed as sweat drenched her face. I snickered at my friend bent over, trying to catch her breath.

"You're such a crybaby. This makes six weeks since you started hiking, and you're worse today than before you started." I grabbed a water bottle out of my backpack and passed it to her.

She hurriedly untwisted the top and downed the water in seconds.

Gretchen wiped her mouth with the back of her hand. "Let me tell you something, Miss Kilimanjaro." I laughed at the dig. "This ain't my ministry. It's yours. I'll stick to the gym from now on. So, don't ask me to come out here no mo'!"

This girl. I shook my head, chuckling. "I didn't ask you. You asked me. Remember you said that you needed to shed those last fifteen pounds of baby weight."

"Why are you bringing up old stuff?"

I laughed at the unserious smirk on her face. "Whatever, but anyway, you've lost ten of the fifteen. Aren't you proud of yourself?"

"I am, but my husband is not. He said he likes the extra weight on me. Me—not so much." She grimaced, shaking her head. "I'll keep the last five pounds for him."

Shaking my head, I gave her a censuring look. "Don't blame quitting on Otis."

"Aye, I'll use whatever excuse to quit," she said with a grin, throwing her hands up. We both laughed.

I agreed with Otis. Gretchen did look good with the extra weight on her. Her stomach was flat, hips wider and breasts fuller. It was the weight in her legs that drove Otis crazy over his wife.

Maybe a baby would put weight on me.

All through school, I was skinny. I got picked on mercilessly, and it didn't help that I didn't have the latest fashions at least to combat the teasing. My mama was a single mother, and she had to work two jobs just to make ends meet. The dollar store and Goodwill were my shopping stores.

Then, I went to college.

I gained the freshman fifteen plus five more. I went from looking a step above emaciated to a luscious, slim. All the boys that teased me sang a new tune once they saw me again. I took pleasure in turning them down.

I evolved. That's why Victor's childish joke about my legs being toothpicks didn't bother me. Besides, I saw interest in his eyes.

Yeah, I saw it and felt it.

Hiding from the truth was never my thing, and I wouldn't start now. I saw the way Victor looked at me. I knew the way I looked at him when he wasn't looking at me. Doing something about it was impossible. I was with Marty, and he was married.

You're both single now.

Gretchen gleefully shared the news two days ago that "my man" was free and clear. And now, I was on high alert. I purposely stayed away from her house.

"Ready to go?" Gretchen's intruding voice halted thoughts of Victor.

"Yep."

We walked back down the incline. On the trek back to my car, we talked about her and Otis joining Sherrie and Owen on their annual month-long trip. They were set to leave next week. I would be in charge of Designed by Sherrie and its three employees while they were gone. Mel and Talik were going too but only for the first two weeks. Talik had to come back to his pastoral duties at Beacon.

"I'm going to miss my Gabby-Gabby and Sunny." Gabby was Gretchen's six-month-old, and Sunny was Sherrie's too cute toddler. They were my babies.

"We'll send pictures of your babies," Gretchen teased, throwing an arm around my shoulders. "I'm sure they'll miss their playmate too."

"Ha, ha, ha." I rolled my eyes at her, shrugging her arm off.

"Tonight is going to be so good. Otis said they're going to do a live tapping of his and Victor's set."

I frowned up. "Why?"

She practically skipped beside me, most likely thinking about her man. Stopping to look around as if looking for lurkers, she whispered, "I'm not supposed to say anything, but Victor is retiring."

"Girl, it's just us out here and animals. Out here whispering." We shared a laugh. "So, he's quitting standup?" I stepped over a fallen tree limb. Any news about Victor, I quickly gobbled it up.

"Yep. He's still gonna dabble in it because he's going continue to write for other comics, but yeah, he's hanging up his microphone."

Wow. He was only forty, which meant he was leaving in his prime.

"I don't know how he deals with Tinashay. You saw what she did the other day?"

I saw it and got angry on Victor's behalf. She was doing the absolute most for clout. Anybody with good sense could see she was doing all the talking, and he wasn't. Clear indication of her guilt. Like my mama always says, "Only the guilty speak."

Homegirl had been speaking since the news dropped about her filing for divorce.

All the headlines featured her, and tea about Victor and his alleged doggish, abusive ways dropped constantly.

He had yet to saying anything about her or address the allegations.

Well...until the press release about him being an ambassador for a dyslexia foundation dropped a couple hours after Tinashay's story about writing his jokes.

Some of the same people that had been dogging him out in the comments on social media since last year were starting to doubt sister girl. But too many still believed her lies.

His friends in comedy were refuting her claims as well about the jokes, and I was happy to see it.

"So, friendddd...." Gretchen began, not waiting on my response to her question seconds ago.

I laughed. "Here you go."

A bright smile lit up her face. "I know you're feeling Victor. If he approaches you tonight, will you be open to dating him?"

I rolled my eyes heavenward.

"Be honest, girl. I know you, and I see the way you clam up and become like a star-struck zombie around him."

"Star-struck zombie? That makes no sense," I said, twisting my lips.

"You know what I mean."

"His divorce is fresh. Newborn fresh. And I'm still messed up over my breakup with Marty." Gretchen's "be for real" glare caused me to fall out laughing. "Okay, Marty aside. Victor just got his final divorce decree two days ago. It's too soon. He needs time to adjust to his new status."

"Blah, blah, blah. Time is irrelevant to this. That man has been separated from that woman for a year. Mind you, he told Otis he'd never get married again and that he was going to be by himself for a while. Tell me why he's talked about you to my husband."

I slapped my stomach to calm the rioting butterflies. "What did he say about me?"

"I guess you'll find out tonight," she cracked, throwing a secretive smile my way.

My mouth gaped open. Nothing came out.

"And don't even think about not coming tonight. Stop being a big scaredy cat and come support my husband and your new man tonight."

Giving her the side-eye, I bit my lip to keep from smiling.

***

My self-care routine was not as enjoyable this time.

I prided myself on lavishing my skin with elixirs, lotions, and creams. Bathtime was an experience. I loved nature, and I equally loved to pamper myself after being outdoors.

My usual routine took two hours, but tonight it took an hour because I skipped steps.

I was nervous.

I can just text Gretchen and say I'm not feeling well.

Standing in my walk-in closet wrapped in a towel, I absentmindedly thumbed through the kaleidoscope ensemble of fashion must-haves. A simple, silk black thin-strapped dress that hit a few inches above my knees caught my attention. Silver accessories would match perfectly. I snatched it off the hook and dropped it on my bed.

My nerves made me unsure of my next steps.

I caught my reflection in the mirror bolted to the wall.

Tension and subdued excitement jumped out at me. Walking closer to stare at myself, I admitted aloud, "I'm not ready for Victor Cole."

Even though scared, I sucked it up and readied myself.

Two hours later, I walked into The Laughing Lounge with my head up high and back straight. I searched the crowd, looking for my people. I jumped at the warm hand on my elbow.

"It's me," Gretchen smiled. "Thought it was your man, huh?"

"You look cute." I waved my hand up and down as I admired her turquoise jumpsuit.

"No, that's all you, honey. You look stunning. The face is beat to perfection, dress fitting like a glove, and the melanin is popping baby. Two snaps up and around the world," Gretchen joked, snapping her fingers.

I laughed, feeling at ease. "You are a mess. Where are we sitting?"

"Upstairs in VIP. You can relax for now. Victor and Otis are backstage doing whatever it is they do to get on stage."

Faking bravado that was slipping by the minute, I waved her off. "Please, I am relaxed."

I followed Gretchen upstairs. The first pair of eyes mine connected to was the one's I hoped was backstage.

And he was in white. My knees automatically weakened, and I had to catch the railing to keep from falling.

A dark chocolate man in white was my kryptonite.

Lord, this man was fine.

Moisturized, beard groomed, tattoos peeping from the pushed-up sleeves of his hoodie, small silver hoop earring in his left earlobe glistening, and his masculinity infusing the room almost made me turn around— that's if my knees would've cooperated.

I watched him.

He watched me.

A slow smile of appreciation crept across he beautiful face.

Fake it 'til you make it.

I produced the haughtiest of glares before stiffly strutting behind my friend to our table. No matter how chocolate and fine he looked, Victor Cole would not break me.

I chanced a look at him, and he mouthed, "Beautiful."

My insides melted.

Ch. 4

Victor

"Thank you, Copeland," fell out of my mouth. Ear-piercing cheers and applause filled the lounge as I walked off the stage. I was anxious to get back to VIP.

I almost broke out into a sweat when Athena topped the stairs.

She was a fine lil' filly prancing around with her skin shimmering in the low light. I flustered her when I mouthed that she was beautiful.

I didn't have time to talk to her because I had to head backstage. Now that my set was over, Athena was all mine.

"Man, I can't believe you're about to give the mic up. What you just did up there was epic," Owen said, dapping me up.

I hesitated to respond because he and Otis, looking like twins, always jarred me for a split second until I remembered they were cousins. "Appreciate it, fam. The stage ain't for me anymore."

Otis dapped me next. "You'll be missed for real."

"You of all people know I'm not going anywhere. I'll be around."

Talik shook my hand next. "Good set, man."

I clasped his hand. Seeing him here in this environment took some getting used to. Not many pastors I knew would go to a comedy lounge without blowback from the church and the community. I guess having all of them muscles deterred anyone from talking too much. Talik was ripped. I wondered how many women called his house under the pretense of needing prayer. He had a dime at home though. All the fellas did. Sherrie was the beautiful girl next door who had all the neighborhood boys in love. Mel was the classy, refined dark beauty who could name all the silverware. Gretchen was the bestie who made her good bro fall in love. They were blessed.

Speaking of, I cast a glance over at the women laughing and talking amongst themselves. I cast my eyes on my blessing.

She was engrossed in whatever they were talking about. I watched her throw her head back and laugh, exposing that beautiful neck of hers.

The fellas converged on the table. Everyone sidled up to their significant other. I slid in the seat next to

Athena, purposely making our bodies touch. Vanilla and coconut assaulted my senses.

Athena stopped midsentence to turn and glare at me. "Excuse you."

"Hey, little filly."

She narrowed her eyes. "I am not a horse."

I grinned a little. "My mistake. It's just your hair made me think otherwise."

She gasped and touched the curly ponytail which obviously wasn't hers. Everybody laughed but her.

She went to move her chair away from mine, but I stayed it with a hand on the leg. "Alright, alright. I'm just playing with you. Dang, beautiful, you make it too easy to mess with you. I like your lil' pony though." I pulled an errant curl and let it bounce back.

A short giggle escaped, before she sobered and rolled her eyes at me.

"Why do you insist on bothering me, Victor Cole?"

I briefly got lost in her slanted eyes before answering. "Because I like messing with you, Athena Rose."

"Ugh, go mess with someone else who wants to be messed with."

"Nah," I shook my head, "I like messing with you."

"Whatever."

"So, what you think?"

Looking confused, she asked, "Think about what?"

"My set." I was anxious to hear what she thought about me, what she thought about my performance.

A slow smile turned her full lips up. "Meh."

"Meh?" I repeated. The grin on my face belied my attempt at being offended.

"I've seen better." Her eyes glittered with mischief.

I laughed loudly at that. "Better than me? Impossible."

"My bro killed it," she said, inclining her head towards Otis without moving her eyes away from mine.

"He ain't me." From my peripheral, I saw Otis grin in response.

That same saccharine smile reappeared as she gloated, "Precisely. He's funny. You're not. I should've at least smirked during your set. I was bored."

A collective "oh!" went around the table before they all laughed.

I leaned closer, and she smirked. "Lying is a sin, Athena. I could practically see your tonsils from the stage." Athena smacked her lips.

"She laughed harder than everybody," Gretchen snitched.

"Gretchen!" The look on her face promised retribution. Gretchen just smiled.

"Mm hm, she did," Mel chimed in.

"You're one of her favorite comedians," Sherrie blurted.

Athena's eyes bulged at the betrayal.

"Stop playing hard to get, sis. The man is clearly interest in you. Both y'all's melanin is popping. He's single, and you're single. What's the problem, Thena?"

"Gret-chen," Athena emphasized between gritted teeth.

"Leave sis alone," Otis chided Gretchen.

"At least Otis has my back," she said, avoiding my eyes.

"Now I can't tell her what I need to tell her because you meddling, Legs." We all looked at him, wondering what he needed to tell Athena.

"Tell me," Athena urged.

"My boy," Otis nodded at me, "wanna holla at you."

Athena busted out laughing along with everyone else. "You are so childish, Otis."

We fist bumped, and she blushed. "Good looking out, bruh."

The waitress showed up with platters of food. My stomach growled when she sat a platter of fried wings and fries down in front of me and Athena. I was starving because I never ate before a show. The last meal I had was at lunchtime.

Talik blessed the food, and we dug in.

Otis and Owen were in a debate about something from their childhood. Talik and Mel were in their own bubble, and Sherrie and Gretchen had their own side conversation. Quiet now, Athena kept her eyes on the plate in front of her.

"Hey," I bumped her arm. Shy eyes peered up at me. "All joking aside, I'm glad you came tonight. You had a brother blushing, knowing I'm your favorite comedian."

"One of my favorites, not *the* favorite."

"Man down. Shots fired," I groaned out, dramatically dropping my chin to my chest.

Giggling, she said, "You are just as childish as Otis."

"But you like it."

Athena bit her lip, eyes shining before answering softly, "A little bit."

"I'll take it."

That was all the encouragement I needed. I spent the remainder of the time teasing her while she threw some humbling zingers my way.

It was a refreshing change.

She was refreshing.

***

Ping. Ping. Ping. Ping. Ping. Ping. Ping.

I snatched the pillow and put it over my head. Soon as I grasped a slice of peace, Shay happened. It started before I went to the club. She pretended that she wanted to know where her birth certificate was.

I ignored the text.

She followed up with: *You must be with your b**ch the reason why you won't answer.*

Like, bruh what? She never used to talk like that. I hated to hear women curse and talk like that. She knew I was serious about my faith now, but she constantly barraged me with this ratchet stupidity.

Ping. Ping. Ping. Ping. Ping. Ping. Ping.

"Oh my...God, please get your girl."

The phone started ringing.

I sat up and snatched my phone off the charger.

2:15 a.m. The late hour glared at me.

I sucked my teeth.

This girl.

If I didn't answer, she'd keep calling. I knew I shouldn't answer, but the quicker I answered and got it out of the way, the faster I could get back to sleep.

"Hello!" I hoped she heard every bit of annoyance in my voice.

Sniffles filled the line.

Negro, why did you answer the phone?

She'd drunk called me again.

"Shay, you gotta stop doing this. It's not healthy for you or for me." I sat up against the head of the bed and waiting to hear her response.

"I'm so sorry, Victor. I'm so sorry," she sobbed into the phone.

I sighed. "I'm sorry too. Our relationship ran its course, Shay, but we have to let go now. I think th—"

"NO! Not the divorce. I'm sorry I couldn't give you babies."

Shay and I tried to have children, but after failed attempts and her refusal to do IVF or adopt, I figured it was God's plan for us not to have any biological children. Our inability to have children never factored into the state of our marriage. Long as I had Shay, I was good. I married her because I loved her, not for her ability to give me kids.

"Listen, that was never a problem for me. I was fine with it being just us."

"No!" she sobbed.

No matter what she'd done and said about me over the last year, I still had compassion for Shay. Her antics could never erase the eighteen years of loving and living we had together. I still had love for her, though I wasn't in love with her anymore.

"Shay, calm down. You're going to make yourself sick."

"I killed him."

Alarm clogged my throat. *Lord, don't tell me this girl was drunk driving.* "Killed who?"

More sobs filled the line.

"Shay!" I yelled to get her attention. I flung back the comforter and sat on the edge of the bed. "Answer me. Who did you kill?"

"Our baby."

What the—

I had to be mistaken. "Shay, what baby?"

"I was pregnant," she cried. "I got rid of it. I made a stupid mistake. I'm so sorry, baby. I wanted to tell you, but VH1 called me to do Love & Hip-Hop. Remember? My storyline as Jezzy's friend wouldn't allow for a baby."

Memories filtered in as a whooshing sound filled my ears. I remembered the tv deal. Tears clouded my eyes as I pieced it all together. Shay's best friend, Jezzy, was on Love & Hip-Hop, and Jezzy decided to bring Shay on the show. I remember right before the show started filming, Shay was at home. She said her cycle had come on and said it was really heavy. I remember her specifically saying she hoped it stopped before she had to start filming.

And I told her it would.

"Shay, no. Tell me..." my voice trailed off. I shook my head in disbelief. Nah, she was lying. She had to be.

"I'm s-s-sorry. Look at your text messages."

I quickly opened the messages from Shay. She'd sent a picture of a sonogram multiple times. I looked at the date.

The image grew blurry as the realization sunk in that she had an abortion.

I dropped the phone and sobbed into my hands.

She killed my baby.

Ch. 5

Athena

I slathered on my coconut scented body scrub up and down my leg.

"Alexa, play the latest Victor Cole video from The Laughing Lounge," I commanded my Echo Dot.

The video's audio began, and I tensed up in anticipation like I wasn't there last night to hear Victor live and in action.

The other night was exciting. Being around Victor was sensory overload, and I couldn't help but be a victim to his charisma, his confidence, his presence.

He was...whew.

Bantering with him stimulated me to the point of surrender. Feigning indifference went out the window soon as he told me he was glad I showed up at the lounge. I *never* felt excitement of that magnitude with Marty. With him, time spent burdened me like it was an obligation. I truly never felt relaxed enough to be around him. Playfully insulting Marty would've been misconstrued and probably would've gotten me a tongue lashing from his mama.

But with Victor, it was fun.

He excited me and relaxed me.

His spirit called out to my spirit.

I have no other way to describe it, but yeah, it's like our spirits recognized one another.

We traded bars for bars, trying to one-up one another, and it felt so darn good to come alive like that. No other man has ever stimulated me like this man.

I actually forgot he was a famous comedian.

Victor was so down to earth and such a chill person. He was confident, which was extremely attractive, and he never played on his celebrity.

However, a deep dive into cyberspace reminded me of his celebrity. And I also forgot about Tinashay. She was in some of his old videos. I skipped those. Then, Alexa tried to be messy by playing one of her videos from her personal channel. I skipped with the quickness. I didn't need thoughts of his ex-love to infiltrate my Victor Cole trance.

Washing the scrub off my legs, I hopped out of the shower and quickly dried off. I'd been so restless since the comedy club that I went for a short solo hike before six just to tire out my nerve endings. It worked. I no longer felt like a livewire.

I also felt some type of way because he asked for my cell number. A number he'd yet to use. But then I also reprimanded myself for thinking that way. The man was busy.

So, in the meantime, I satisfied myself with thoughts of him to keep my mind distracted from the fact he hadn't called me.

Victor stayed on my brain, and this man had me talking to God about him all giggly and whatnot, like I was gushing to my bestie about my teen crush. God didn't mind. He knew everything I was thinking and feeling anyway.

I eased down on the stool in front of my bathroom vanity and pulled out my coconut vanilla body cream. Just as I opened the top, my phone rang.

"Alexa, answer the phone." I waited a second, hearing the background noise of someone traveling. "Hello?"

"Good morning, Athena."

I jerked at the smooth baritone flowing through the Echo Dot's speaker. I clasped my towel as if this man could see me in my state of undress through the phone. My actions caused me to knock over my jar of cream. A small amount of its contents splattered on my foot.

"Aw, shoot!"

"What's wrong? What happened?" His protective tone said he was ready to ride to my rescue.

I liked that.

A lot.

Blushing, I stuttered, "N-nothing. I dropped something."

"Okay." He sounded relieved. "I thought I was gonna have to play Superman this morning."

I grinned at the thought. Making quick cleanup of the spilled cream, I responded, "I'm more partial to the caped crusader."

"Oh, so you have a thing for Batman?"

I grinned harder. "It's something about seeing a confident man in all black fighting villains with his human strength. That's a real man."

"Did you hear on the news about the man who fought ten drug dealers with his bare hands?"

"Um, no. When and where did this happen?" I questioned through a laugh.

"Right here in Mayberry last night."

I playfully fussed at him, "Leave my town alone."

"I have affection for Mayberry, but anyway, this dude was wearing an all-black LaQuan Smith suit when he straight mollywhopped all ten of them fools. They also say his suit jacket looked like a cape."

"Oh really? He sounds like a man I need to get to know. I wonder who he is and what's his story." My smiling face in the mirror caught my attention. The joy on my face made me blush again.

His lazy West Coast drawl eased out, "I normally keep Black Ninja's identity a secret, but I'll tell you." He paused dramatically. In a deep voice, he growled out, "I'm Black Ninja."

I cracked up, and his chuckle joined in.

"I'm not fooling with you this early in the morning, Black Ninja. Speaking of morning, why are you up so early?"

"I had some business to take care of, and I called you because I wanted to hear your voice. I would've called yesterday, but some...something came up." His pause before saying "something" felt off.

"Are you okay today?" I asked, knowing whatever it could be was still bothering him.

He sighed before answering. "I will be."

Guess me and God was about to have another tête-à-tête about his son.

"I know we barely know one another, but anytime you want to talk, I'm here," I offered.

"Raincheck?"

"Of course."

"Hey, I gotta go. I called to see if you were coming to the community center tonight. I want to see you."

Biting my lip, I did a mean shimmy.

"I'll be there. Since all my friends are leaving me behind, they're trying to placate me with free food and games. I mean, it's working, but I don't wanna be left behind."

"I'll be here for a while. We can hang. I won't allow you to be alone."

I can have you all to myself, and what's a while?

"I'd like that."

"Hey, I gotta go. See you later?"

Hoping the disappointment of our conversation ending so soon didn't come across, I answered with an upbeat, "Yep, later."

"Have a good day at work, Athena."

"Thanks, and you and Black Ninja have a good day."

He laughed. "We'll do our best."

I made sure the Echo Dot ended the call. I stared at myself in the mirror and palmed my hot cheeks as they spread out into the biggest smile.

Eventually, I forcefully pulled myself from La-la land and finished my skincare routine. I hurried to the kitchen and whipped up a veggie omelet. An hour later, I was out the door and in my car headed to work.

Thoughts of Victor followed me throughout the day.

***

He was late or probably not coming at all. My eyes went to the entrance to the play center repeatedly since I got here and realized he wasn't here.

Otis was mum about his whereabouts, and I was too embarrassed to ask where his friend was. And I was embarrassed by how disappointed I was that he wasn't here. I needed to get my emotions in check.

Girl, your enjoyment tonight is not contingent on his presence. Enjoy your night, I told myself. I shook off the discontent.

Sherrie was beginning to eat after feeding Sunny, and Gretchen was feeding Gabby. I contemplated asking Mel to come play a game with me. Nah, she was too busy all up under her man. Otis and Owen had inhaled their food already and were in the small gym on the other side of the center.

I announced, "Y'all, I'm going to play."

Gretchen looked up. "I'll meet you in thirty."

"Okay."

I played a few games before a familiar voice interrupted my fun.

Marty stood awkwardly looking at me. A pretty woman, brown skinned woman stood directly behind him.

"Fancy seeing you here."

Yeah, fancy that. Marty was either too dumb or too stupid to approach me while on a date with another woman. We'd just broke up less than two weeks ago. And he'd never brought me to an arcade much less done anything fun with me.

I got the stale dates with his mama.

Now after he broke up with me, he wanted to get some seasoning in his life.

I stood there feeling insulted.

"Fancy seeing *you* here," I mimicked him with an attitude. Pursing my lips, I folded my arms and cocked my hip to the side. The universal black woman with an attitude stance.

"I...ah...I saw you and wanted to say hello," he stammered. His date's face remained serene.

"You wanted to say hello to me while you're on a date," I murmured contemplatively, looking up at the ceiling for a moment, then returned my glare back on him. "Why?"

"I figured there shouldn't be any hard feelings."

This fool was crazy. I started to unleash on him, but the hairs on my arms stood up.

Victor.

Seconds later, a muscled arm snaked around my waist and a warm pair of lips touched the side of my neck.

"Jesus..." hissed between my teeth.

"Nah," he whispered in my ear causing goosebumps to pop up on my skin in response. "Black Ninja to the rescue."

A giggle burst out.

"Take a ride with me." That wasn't a question.

"Sure," I agreed.

We walked away, leaving Marty and his date.

***

We rode in silence the first mile until he cashed in his raincheck.

I learned what the "something" was that he was obviously bothered by this morning when we talked.

I listened and didn't interrupt.

D'Angelo's "Cruisin'" played softly in the background.

I absorbed his visible pain as he told me about the baby.

About Shay and her duplicity.

Anger and grief radiated off him, but the grief surpassed the anger.

The urge to touch him engulfed me, and I reached across the console and grabbed his hand. He stopped midsentence and turned to me.

I told him to pull over.

Once the car came to a stop, I immediately interceded on his behalf.

Seconds turned into minutes as I asked God to soothe his heart, to help him grieve the way he needed, to know who he was in Him, to rest in Him, to not become cold so he wouldn't have to carry the weight of someone else's sin and so he'd be able to walk in freedom knowing he wasn't guilty.

I opened my eyes to find his waiting.

And...we stared.

We stared at one another, visually tethering our emotions.

Both of us sat still, powerless to break our connection. It was so intense. My senses were overloaded, and I struggled to keep from drowning in them. I took deep, silent breaths to allow the currents to flow unimpeded between us.

I don't know how long we sat there staring at one another. Could've been a few seconds or minutes. The calculation of time escaped me.

Eventually, he spoke.

"Did you just get me emotionally drunk?"

Feeling inebriated myself, I could only shrug.

Ch. 6

Victor

A meeting of the minds commenced in Otis's media room.

Marianna and my manager Heath were on the big monitor as well as O's manager Vlad. We were doing a three-hour taped special. Basically, it was going to be a collaboration slash retirement party in L.A. It was all O's idea, and I loved it. Heath pitched it to Amazon Prime, and they accepted. The plan was for me to headline, and O would be the major act before me. A few heavy hitters signed on to do an hour-long roast. I gave Heath strict instructions for them to keep is as PG as possible. My parents, my pastor, and my people from here would be there.

"Shelia Vee confirmed the venue, caterer, and decorations. She says the old Hollywood theme has been added to the invites," Marianna read off the list she held up.

Heath spoke next. "Mari suggested using social media influencers in the weeks leading up to the event to market the special. I think that's genius.

Everyone is on social media now. Even me." Heath was an old head with plenty of experience in the game. Him on social media wasn't a shock. Bruh was nosy, so it made sense.

"Yes!" Marianna chirped. "Thanks for reminding me, Heath. I have a list of influencers that I need you to look over."

I closed my eyes in resignation. I hated social media, and I only had accounts to post promo for events and stuff. I let the social media manager Marianna hired be the one to post most of the content. A few selfies from me occasionally made their way to IG.

"No whining, Victor. I also suggest you two do a few skits. People love skits on social media."

"Who is you two?" Otis asked, looking perturbed. He hated social media worse than I did.

Vlad laughed before saying, "You, Otis. This will be great and will give you even more exposure. Gotta do what you gotta do in this business to stay relevant, my man. Think of this event as Victor passing the torch to you."

"This old negro passing the torch with them shaky hands?" Otis smirked, and we all laughed. "Yeah, alright."

"Y'all done with this update?" I asked Marianna, ready to get out of this meeting.

"Sure, crybaby. We'll let you go and finish the planning amongst ourselves."

Otis reached over to the computer. "Say less." This fool cut the feed.

I laughed at him. "O, man you didn't give them the opportunity to say goodbye. You just cut the feed."

He shrugged, unrepentant. "They didn't need us. Everything they told us could've been in said in a text message."

I just shook my head.

"Ay man, you sure you good staying here by yourself?"

I frowned at him. "I'm a grown man."

Otis laughed before throwing up his hands. "I meant that we're leaving after I invited you here."

"Nah, I'm good," I assured him. "I'm enjoying Mayberry more than I thought. I'm meeting with a realtor today to go look at houses."

"Man, same thing happened to me. I came to Copeland and couldn't find my way back to Chicago if I wanted to. It's something special about this place I don't want to let go of."

Shooting him a dubious look, I said, "Special meaning Gretchen."

A broad smile covered his face. "Well yeah. It was the legs."

"Simp." I threw the insult at him.

"Takes one to know one." He toasted me with his water bottle.

"Touché, simpleton, touché."

"When you meeting the realtor?" Otis asked, standing up and stretching.

I looked at my Apple watch. "In an hour. I already know the house I want to see."

"You got time for breakfast. Legs put some pancakes, sausage and eggs in the warmer."

I beat Otis downstairs. My stomach was on empty after my early morning workout. I quickly fixed my plate and gave God his props before I dug in.

"This house you buying…" Otis paused to douse his pancakes in syrup. "Does my sis have sway?"

"All the sway."

"You for real on this *meet me at the altar in your white dress*," he sang, and I laughed.

"For real, O. Last night sealed it for me." I filled my mouth with eggs.

I shook my head, remembering how drunk I was off Athena.

Not a drop of liquor was involved.

That had never happened to me before.

Drunk off emotions because of a woman? Nah, never, but I was ready to get drunk again.

After me and Athena came up missing from the community center, Otis and Gretchen called our phones at the same time. I gave him a brief rundown of what happened when I got back to his house.

"Listen, a praying woman is a keeper. I get it because Legs helped me overcome my panic attacks. Athena is a good woman. Protect her because Shay is going to lose her mind when she finds out about her...with her foul behind." He knew about the baby too.

Swallowing my food and swallowing the anger trying to rise, I addressed his concern. "I know. I need to make my intentions clear with Athena, and I won't sugarcoat my situation with Shay. Maybe she'll leave me alone now that her conscience is clear."

"Maybe," he said, unconvincingly.

Yeah, maybe, but I had a feeling that Shay was just getting started.

***

"Hey Victor," Sherrie greeted.

"How you doing'?" I hugged her.

"I feel good." She looked good too in her high waisted shorts, putting her legs on display. A brief thought crossed my mind. Her, Mel, Gretchen, and Athena all had nice legs. Perhaps great legs were a prerequisite to their friendship circle.

"Where's my girl?"

Sherrie beamed, clapping her hands, making me laugh at her exuberance. "Y'all are so cute together. She's over there." I followed her finger to the left side of the store to see Athena going through a rack of clothes. "Tell her she can take two hours for lunch."

I eased up behind Athena and whispered in her ear. "Guess who?"

"Black Ninja," she answered.

"Shhh...people are listening. I'm just Vic today."

She turned around, and we automatically fell into a hug. I wanted to kiss her neck like last night but refrained. Last night was necessary though. I enjoyed seeing the anger and defeat on Marty's face.

"You smell nice," she complimented. My heart sped up at the happiness I saw on her face.

"You do too. I love this." I fingered the feminine short set she was wearing.

She blushed. "Thanks."

"I'm here to take you to lunch. We need to talk."

"Okay, let me tell Sherrie—"

"Already done. I got you for two hours."

"Look at you being all proactive," she teased. "I need my purse."

I shook my head. "No, you don't. I got you. Whenever you're with me, you won't need to touch your wallet. And..." I held up a finger to halt the ready argument on her lips. "It's not about gender roles or me having my way. It's about pampering you. Can I pamper you, Athena?"

Her face softened. "Yes, you can pamper me, Victor."

We went to the comedy club since I knew no one but staff would be there. She and I would be able to talk uninterrupted. I paid one of the waitresses to put a tablecloth on the table and a bouquet of flowers.

"These are nice." Athena smiled softly, smelling the mix of roses and sunflowers. "Thank you."

"A little birdie told me you love soft tacos," I said as I pulled the shrimp and beef tacos out of the picnic basket the waitress left on the chair close to our table. Athena's eyes lit up.

"Are you trying to make me fall in love with you?" She asked, now inhaling the aroma of the tacos.

"That's the plan."

Her eyes snapped up to mine in surprise.

"I was just joking."

"I'm not." I was serious. I was right on the edge of falling. Another blush or smile from her could easily push me over the edge.

"I don't know what to say," she said, fidgeting with her silverware.

"Athena." She looked up. Fear and yearning looked back at me. "I'm a man about my business. I don't believe in beating around the bush. Being real is the only way I know how to be. Can you accept that from me and give me that in return? If not, I'll accept that and take my time with you until you can accept it."

She exhaled shakily. "I can accept it." Athena looked away for a second. "I want to be real with you too."

"The thought of you makes my heart beat faster, so you can imagine how it beats when I'm in your presence. The first time I met you, I was messed up, but I saw you. I think you're beautiful inside and out, and I feel at home when I'm around you."

"Victor...ar-are you asking to be my man?"

"I'm telling you I'm going to be your man."

She laughed, relaxing in her seat. "Oh, so I don't have a say?"

"Nope."

"Okay. Promise me if you decide that you're interested in someone else, don't waste my time and string me along. Tell me up front."

Interested in someone else? Impossible.

"I'm not Martian."

She choked on a laugh. "Marty."

"I said what I said." I shrugged, then shared, "I just put in an offer on a house in O's neighborhood."

She got my meaning. Our eyes locked, and another link in our emotional tethering added to the thickening strand.

I broke eye contact to fix her plate. "Tell me about your work."

She startled as if remembering that we were supposed to be eating lunch. I passed her the plate, and she murmured her thanks.

I said a quick prayer.

Athena shared that she went to Belhaven University and graduated with a degree in Fashion Merchandizing. Her love of fashion came from not having the latest fashions during her school years because her and her mother struggled financially. Her father died before Athena was born, so her mother didn't have help with her rearing. After working for Dillard's for a few years, she found out about Sherrie's shop and moved from Jackson to Copeland. Gretchen followed not long after.

"I do a lot of consulting instore and virtually as well as liaising with designers so Designed by Sherrie can carry their clothes. We were a little skeptical at first to do that because Copeland is a small town, but people from surrounding areas with a few dollars in their pocketbooks have made the venture a big success."

"You love what you do," I said, admiring the passionate glint in her eyes. She was truly never more beautiful sitting here talking about the purpose in her life.

She dipped her fork into the slice of carrot cake I brought for dessert. "I do. What about you? What are you passionate about?"

I thought for a second. "I'm passionate about being a hands-on ambassador for TDF. I personally know how confusing and insecure a child can feel when faced with dyslexia. Before the diagnosis, a child believes they're stupid and something is wrong with them. That's a big burden on small shoulders."

"I can imagine it is."

"I try to bridge the gap for the kids with their confidence and coping mechanisms by sharing my story and helping them realize that nothing is wrong with them. Plus, if I can conquer dyslexia, they can too."

"I love that." Athena smiled like a proud parent.

Conversation switched to my business endeavors. I told her about being a spokesman for a Black owned jewelry company. I showed her the watch on my wrist. She fawned over it, saying she wanted one too. I made a mental note to get the feminine version and have it shipped to Copeland asap.

"You, Owen, and Otis have helped Copeland's economy so much. The vegan restaurant is a nice touch. I'm a tiny bit vegan, mostly carnivore, but I enjoy the vegan burgers a lot. They taste like the real deal. I promise, I never thought it could be done, but y'all did it."

I laughed and nodded, knowing what she was talking about. "My brother, Mason, got me hooked on them. He was like, 'Bro, they taste like real hamburgers.' I tried one, and six months later, I opened my own restaurant in L.A., then Chicago, then Miami, and now Copeland. Health is literally wealth, and I'm glad I cashed in on it."

"That's something to think about. I'm a girly girl, but I love the outdoors. I should look into workout clothes for the outdoors." At my questioning look, because she had the uncanny skill to read my mind, she explained, "I try to hike every weekend, and once a year, I go camping. Not glamping but real roughing it type deal."

"I never imagined hiking or camping coming out of your mouth."

She let loose a gleeful laugh. "Nature is one of my happy places. I used to get my mother to take me. She's long abandoned me, and my girls absolutely won't go unless there's electricity and a working shower and toilet. So, I sign up every year for this group for singles who camp, and we go camping together. I've met a lot of nice people."

"Count me in on the next camping trip."

"Seriously? Don't play with me, man." Athena bounced in her seat.

I grinned at her enthusiasm. She was so cute. "Seriously. Take me on your next hike too."

"Finally, Lord. I have a partner in crime," she burst out, waving her hand, making me laugh again.

I saluted her. "Black Ninja to the rescue once again."

She exaggeratedly batted her eyelashes. "My hero."

Ch. 7

Athena

"Hey, Ma!" I hollered as I stepped into my childhood home.

"Guh, stop all that hollering when you come in here. I ain't deaf." Chelsea Rose rounded the corner with a frown.

"You know you're getting old and them ears are not the same," I said, poking fun.

"I have you to know that I have bionic ears," she fussed, swiping her hand at me.

I dodged the blow with a laugh and swooped in to give my favorite girl a bear hug.

Hugs from my mama never got old.

"Hey, my baby, I missed you," she said, planting kisses all over my face. I sighed contentedly, engaging in our decades-long routine of hugs and kisses.

"I missed you too." That's why I drove up to Jackson today. The last time we saw one another was two weeks ago. We talked every other day, but I needed to see her beautiful face.

I pulled back to look my mama up and down. She was too cute in her sundress.

"Where you going looking like a snack, Miss Thing?"

She chortled, dragging me along with her to the living room. "I just got back from brunch with my sister circle."

"Had all of them AARP members looking at you, huh?" I said, flopping down on the sofa.

"Guh, please. I don't have time for a man, and speaking of...what's his name?"

"Huh?" She just changed up on me right quick.

Making an aha face while circling her finger in my direction, she said, "I see a glow. I know my child, and I know a glow when I see one. What is this man's name you've failed to tell me about?"

Lord, I really believe my mama is psychic. Story of my life because I could never get away with anything growing up. She always knew when I got out of pocket.

"His name is Victor Cole. We've only been dating for about a few weeks."

"Victor Cole...Victor Cole...I know that name," she mused.

I helped her out. "He's the comedian you said was a chocolate dream boat. The one who Otis did that Netflix special with."

"Oh!" Her eyes lit up in recognition. "You're dating him? What about Marty? I thought Victor Cole was married. Young lady, I know you're not being a side item."

I busted out laughing. "You mean sidepiece, and no, I'm not. He is divorced. Also, Marty and I broke up a while ago. His mama made the decision for him."

"That ol' hag. I say good riddance. No woman wants a wimp for a man."

True that.

I gave her a brief synopsis of my new relationship. My mama cheesed the whole time as I explained how Victor made me feel compared to the flaccid emotions Marty elicited.

"My baby," Mama cried, yanking me into her arms again. "I'm so happy for you. This Victor is the one. I can feel it."

"I think you're jumping the gun, ma'am." I wanted Victor to be the one, but God needed to confirm before I forever claimed him.

"Have I ever told you anything wrong?"

I thought for a second. "Umm yeah, when I asked you to bump my ends in the eighth grade, and you gave me them tight grandmother curls you said would drop by the time I went to school. They didn't. I got clowned all day. Everybody called me Mother Athena."

Giving me a pop on my leg, she side-eyed me. "I'm not talking about that frivolous example." *Frivolous?* "I'm talking about life lessons that matter. I've always used the Word and my God-given discernment to steer you in the right direction. Once again, I ask. Have I ever told you anything wrong?"

Mama was right. "No ma'am."

My phone rang.

Oh, shoot. I forgot that I was supposed to text Victor when I made it. He was in a meeting before I left Copeland, but he instructed me to text him when I arrived.

"Hey, I was just about to text you," I lied.

"Umm hmm," he said dryly, and I giggled.

"I'm sorry," I said, laughing. "I forgot. Me and Mama been in here talking."

"Talking about you!" she hollered. I mouthed for her to hush, and she loud-capped me. "You don't tell me to hush, guh. You in my house, and I'll talk as long and loud as I want to talk."

Victor was laughing on the other end of the phone. I shook my head at my feisty mama. Acting out because she knew Victor was on the phone.

"Let me talk to him." She stuck her hand out.

I sighed, mumbling into the phone, "Victor, my mama wants to talk to y—"

The phone was snatched out of my hand before I could finish my sentence.

"Victor Cole..." her voice trailed off as she quickly hustled out of the living room. I knew what she was doing, getting alone so I couldn't hear her ask invasive questions.

I waited for ten minutes before seeking her out. I found her in her room on the bed crying with my phone up to her ear. Alarmed, I hurried over.

"That's beautiful, Victor. You have my blessing." She sniffled and dabbed at her eyes. Reaching for my hand, she pulled me down beside her and blew me a kiss.

I relaxed.

The conversation continued a few more minutes before Mama said, "I'll tell her. It was nice talking to you, Victor. You come to see me soon, okay? Okay.

Yeah, me too. I can't wait to meet you too. Ha, ha, ha. She is." Mama peeped at me, and I frowned, wondering what was being said. "You know her well already." More laughter and finally, "Have a good meeting, sweetie. Bye." She ended the call.

"What did y'all talk about?"

She tweaked my nose. "None of your business. That's between me and my future son."

"Uh, turning against your daughter for a man you haven't met. The betrayal."

The rest of the visit with my mama was fun. She made me go into the kitchen with her to help her cook so I could take back the leftovers. I left a few hours later laden with containers for the week.

***

"Knock, knock," I said, holding up a bag with a container of food.

Victor's smile always did something to me. It was like pure sunshine that warmed the body inside and out.

He opened the door wearing basketball shorts and a plain white tee, looking relaxed and manly at the same time.

"You made it home to me, I see." We shared a hug, and he placed a lingering kiss on my forehead. I loved his forehead kisses.

"And bearing gifts. Ma sent you seared salmon over rice pilaf with a side of broccoli."

He grinned, kissing a dent into my cheek. "Aww man, it smells good too. I'm about to heat this bad boy up right now."

After heating the food, I followed him into the media room. I did a doubletake at the ball of yarn and crochet needle sitting in one of the recliners.

"Ummm.... what's up with the needle and yarn?" I sat on the other side of Victor.

He was tearing into the food. "That's mine," he garbled.

My eyebrows went sky high. "You-you knit?" I was tickled.

"No, I crochet. It soothes me." He was oblivious to my mirth.

My mouth dropped open. Jokes for days danced across my mind.

"I knew you were older than me, but not that old. Black don't crack, Mr. Cole," I said on a giggle.

He smirked, closing the container. "Filly, don't make me snatch that ponytail."

"You better not touch my hair," I threatened as I continued to laugh.

I squealed in laughter when he pounced on me suddenly. We play wrestled until I gave in.

Still laughing and out of breath, I asked him to explain to me how he got into crocheting. His publicist's grandmother taught him to help him combat anxiety and stress. He'd crocheted over fifty blankets and beanie hats. As he was explaining, I admired how he didn't feel any shame about his hobby. He even whipped out his phone to show me pictures of the blankets and hats. I couldn't lie, I was impressed.

"Can you crochet a hat like this for me?" I asked, showing him a ruffled crochet hat with a sunflower design on my phone.

"After you just laughed at me. You don't deserve my creations." He playfully snatched away from me.

"Aww, come on. Don't be like that. What would Black Ninja do?" I cracked up.

"Now you're really not getting one."

"Okay, okay." I wrapped my arms around him. "Make me one. Pretty please, Victor Wictor."

He smiled and dropped a kiss on my temple. "You think because you bat those beautiful eyes and talk in that baby voice that I'll give in." I gave him puppy dog eyes. He laughed. "You can get that, beautiful."

"Yay!"

"Hold up a second." I moved back and watched Victor pull out an oblong jewelry box from between the recliner's cushions. "This is for you."

Intrigued, I opened the box and gasped. It was the feminine version of the watch I admired during lunch the other week.

"Victor," I breathed out, touching the sleek watch. "This is beautiful."

"Let me put it on." He smoothly clasped the watch around my wrist, then put his wrist beside mine. "Now we match."

I was completely surprised by the thoughtful gesture. "Thank you, Victor."

No man had ever given me a gift just because and without strings attached. Marty sucked at giving gifts. For my birthday, he bought me a gift that his mother liked. I ended up giving it to her.

Victor just didn't know. I was about to match his energy. I'd been waiting a long time for someone I could match energies with.

***

Thirty minutes into the movie Victor put on, his phone started pinging back-to-back. He sighed the most tired sigh I ever heard.

"Who is it?"

"Shay."

My thoughts screeched to a halt.

The other week at lunch, Victor explained his situation with Tinashay. I got the good, the bad, and the ugly. He didn't place blame or point fingers; he just told the unadulterated truth. He even showed me proof of her infidelity, the bi-polar text messages and all. He hid nothing, and I appreciated him for not keeping me in the dark.

He promised to keep me away from her shenanigans.

"See what she wants."

Shaking his head vehemently, Victor turned his phone down. "I don't have the energy to deal with her tonight. This is our time, and I want us to continue to enjoy ourselves without the influence of outside forces. Shay is more than likely drunk texting again."

"Okay."

He looked surprised by my easy acquiescence. "Okay?"

I smiled at him. "Okay. You're protecting our peace. I'm okay with it."

He leaned over and kissed me softly on the lips. Our first kiss was quick but potent. "You make it so easy," he murmured against my lips.

"Whatever that means."

"You're not ready for that yet."

I shrugged off my curiosity, and we continued the movie.

***

A new headline dominated social media the next morning: COMEDIAN VICTOR COLE FORCES EX-WIFE TO ABORT THEIR CHILD.

Ch. 8

Victor

I missed Athena.

I missed her calming presence. I missed her knowing just the right thing to say or do when I was anxious about the planning of my upcoming show. The incomplete feeling I had whenever we were apart followed me all this week as I traveled for work.

I went to New York for an early morning interview with The Breakfast Club. They tried to slip in questions about Shay's "abortion." Everybody had something to say about a marriage they didn't have firsthand knowledge of. I was tired of it. I made it clear that if they didn't have questions about my retirement and my last show, I was gone go mute on them for the rest of the interview.

Anyway, my next stop was Miami so I could check in on my investments, and then, I jetted to L.A. to film two commercials for a new internet service taking over the West Coast.

Once I finished filming, I rode over to Marianna's office so she and I could strategize my next steps concerning my retirement. She suggested I go back to my old stomping grounds to surprise the audience. I thought that was cool and told her to quickly set that up for a few months out.

"Vic, your driver is here," Pristly, Marianna's assistant, announced.

"Thanks, Pris." I hugged Marianna. "Preciate all your hard work."

"You know it's my pleasure, Victor."

I almost forgot. I pulled the envelope out of my hoodie and passed it to Marianna. "This is Soph's birthday money. Tell her Uncle Vic said not to spend it all in one place."

Marianna laughed. "Sophia is certainly going to ignore that advice."

"Like mother, like daughter. I'm out."

Soon as I made it outside, I texted Athena. Throughout my day, no matter what I did, I sent her *just thinking of you* texts or crazy stuff to make her laugh. I wanted her to know she was always on my mind.

I hopped into the blacked-out SUV and told JB, my driver, to take me to my parents' home. I made a quick phone call to Veg Out to order Athena a cheeseburger with sweet potato fries and a tumbler with her favorite strawberry watermelon drink. The manager, Carrie, promised to personally deliver the food to my girl.

Ping. Ping. Ping. Ping. Ping.

"It never freaking ends," I growled.

JB shook his head. "Man, couldn't be me. I would've aired ol' girl out long time ago."

"Believe me I want to, JB, but God got me on mute indefinitely." I dropped my head back against the headrest.

"God taking too long." JB shook his head.

"His timing is perfect. I refuse to go before Him and mess up what's He's doing on my behalf. Keeping quiet ain't easy, but the consequences of my disobedience will be worse."

He gave me a stare of admiration.

"You a real one, bruh. I respect it."

JB and I were the same age. After several run-ins with the law and the death of his neighborhood friends over the years and a twenty-year bid, he finally made a change. That change led him to meet my brother, Mason, who owned a lucrative janitorial service. Mason hired him at first and quickly realized thereafter the job didn't fit. Lil' bro referred him to me, and I hired him right on the spot.

As my loyal driver for the past eight years, JB knew the good, the bad, and the ugly between me and Shay. He was the one who hipped me to Shay's affair with the brother of one of her ratchet friends.

A text came through from Athena. I opened it and smiled at the kiss and heart eyes emojis along with thanks in all caps. I quickly responded; **Gotta take care of mine.**

My phone buzzed immediately. ***I know that's right Black Ninja. Gotta meeting in five. Call me later.***

Will do, Filly.

LOL! You are not funny. G'Bye!

Talk later baby.

I was still smiling to myself when my phone rang.

"Why is he calling me?" I asked out loud.

JB said over his shoulder as he switched lanes, "Who dat?"

"My lawyer." Lawrence Thomas was my divorce lawyer. His fees were paid, and the case was over. Why was he calling me? "What's up, Lawrence?"

"Vic, my man, how you been?"

"It's all good."

"Good, good. Mrs. Cole called my office earlier this morning. She said she's been calling you about your personal effects that needs to be picked up, but you won't answer her calls. Instead of calling you again, she said she'd get me to pass the message on."

I scrubbed a hand down my face. I did *not* want to go to that house again. I hadn't been there since I moved most of my stuff out when we first separated.

And I most definitely did not want to see Shay or hear her voice. The social media revenge tour was enough for me.

I debated on whether I needed the last few boxes of clothes, awards, and scrap books.

"Mrs. Cole assured me she wouldn't be at home. You still have a key to the home?"

"Yeah."

"Perfect. Get in and get out as fast as possible, and you will be officially done."

I was officially done now.

Except I wanted my belongings.

"Aye, take me to the crib," I told JB after hanging up with Lawrence. He gave me a quick, questioning glare before returning his eyes to the road. I answered, "Shay ain't there, and I need to pick up the rest of my stuff, that's if she ain't damaged it."

JB tsked, "I wouldn't put it past her."

Twenty minutes later, we pulled into the circular driveway of my former home. I looked up at the four-thousand square foot home—the home that used to be my dream home—remembering the good days me and Shay had. Life was good until a few years ago when she decided she wanted fame more than me and more than living for God. That's when our marriage started crumbling into dust. For me, I prayed about it, suggested therapy, initiated communication, and tried date nights, but I caved when Shay presented me with divorce papers.

Man, we used to be a team. We had each other's backs through the hard times. The beginning of my career and having to pinch pennies while eating noodles and bologna sandwiches. Her failed acting career because she wasn't consistent.

The miscarriages.

All five of them.

Giving up never crossed my mind until she cheated.

JB opening his door knocked me out of my reverie. I took a deep breath before following.

"Don't look like anybody is here. I suggest we get in and get out as fast as we can cause I ain't trying to be in no drama."

I frowned at JB. "You say it like I'm trying to be in some."

"You know what I mean, Vic."

"Come on with yo' scary..." I looked at him in disappointment and smirked. "Big giant scared of a woman half his size. Ya' hate to see it."

He laughed. "Vic, gone with that. Shay don't scare me."

"Yeah," I said, laughing too.

I used my key to unlock the door. I put up a mental block as I moved through the house and up the stairs to room that used to be my man cave. Soon as I opened the door, I was met with totally different décor. She'd turned my man cave into some froufrou crap that, peeping the big ring light attached to the ceiling, must be where she was now filming for her YouTube channel. When we filmed together, we utilized the entire house.

But that was over too.

I created my own channel right before we separated.

"Man, look at dis," JB said, looking disgusted at the room. "She cross-dressed your man cave."

I busted out laughing. "Fool."

"Where the boxes at?"

I looked around at the glitz and glam clutter-free room. "She must've put them in the garage."

We retraced our steps and hustled across the house to the four-car garage. The G-Wagon I bought Shay two years ago sat in its spot. Her Audi was missing. I quickly located the boxes. I opened the flaps on all seven boxes, expelling a sigh of relief that all my stuff was unharmed.

"All these are mine," I told JB, pointing at the boxes on the shelf.

I jogged over and pressed the button for the garage door closest to us. We carried two at a time to speed up the process. On the trip back in, my stomach clenched at the sound of car doors closing. Me and JB looked at one another and sped to the boxes. The remaining doors opened, and Shay's screeching voice filled the garage.

"What are you doing in my house? I know you ain't stealing from me, Vic." Shay, in all her Botox-BBL-breast-implant glory, sauntered into the garage with her ratchet friend and film crew. Even with all the work she had done, my ex-wife was still a beautiful woman.

JB folded his arms, looking aggressive. He mumbled my way, "This girl buggin' for real. Call that lawyer so the cameras can see she ain't nothing but a liar."

I did just that and called Lawrence while Shay and her friend squawked in the background.

"Victor, you a lying piece of crap," Treshon said, rushing me as I waited for the phone to connect.

"Back up!" JB moved in front of me, pushing her back with his body.

"Don't touch her! How about I call the police and have you and your driver arrested for assault and trespassing? You just don't know how to stay away. Just leave me a-a..." her voice broke. Tears crested in her eyes and spilled over.

I couldn't believe the performance she was putting on.

I almost told her if she had put this much discipline into them auditions, maybe she'd have an acting career.

I peeped the camera crew eating the drama up. My neck was tight with tension. It was taking a considerable amount of control not to snap.

Finally answering his phone, I spat out, "Aye Lawrence, you're on speakerphone. Say what you told me about coming to get my stuff."

Shay's panicked face turned to me before checking to see if the cameraman saw what I was doing. "Uh-uh, Treshon, let's go. I can't stand to be around him right now."

Her friend snatched away, pointing her long, ugly nails at me. "No, I can't stand these trash Black men getting away with hurting good Black women. Black women need to be protected!" she yelled my way.

I rolled my eyes at the same time JB yelled for her to shut up.

"Hello?" Lawrence had to be confused by all the noise, so I repeated myself and walked closer to the camera crew. "Oh, Mrs. Cole asked that you come over to the house and pick up your belongings while she was away from home."

Staring straight at Shay, I asked him, "When did she call you?"

"She called me over an hour ago. She said she had an appointment and filming until about three p.m., and the house would be clear for you to go in and get your things."

"So, I'm not trespassing?" I watched as Treshon's confused face turned to Shay, who was looking rattled.

"No, you're not trespassing when you have a key and Mrs. Cole gave permission for you to enter the premises."

I smirked at the camera. "Thanks, Lawrence."

"Anytime."

I head motioned at JB to resume getting the boxes. I grabbed the last one and proceeded to walk out of the garage without giving Shay or her friend the satisfaction of a direct response from me.

I smiled at the silence behind me.

***

I spent a few days with my family before hopping back on a plane to Copeland. My family had my heart, and I enjoyed spending time with my parents and my brother. We caught up on things we'd missed since I left to vacation in Mississippi.

Ma tripped on me again about marrying Shay all those years ago, and she straight went off when I told her what happened at the house. To be fair, she did tell me not to marry Shay.

My dad was the same as always. Me, him, and Mason were able to get in a guys' outing without my mama and my sister-in-law, Faith.

Mason and Faith announced they were expecting. She was six months already. They were able to hide her pregnancy since she was carrying small. Mason explained that they waited to tell us because of complications the first few months. I mentally checked to see if I felt a way about the announcement, well in terms of grief, but I felt nothing but joy for them.

It was a good time.

But I was ready to see my lil' filly.

Ch. 9

Athena

"Daddy Randall!" I squealed, hugging Gretchen's father after opening the door to find him standing there dressed to impress.

"Hey, baby girl." He pulled back to peer at me. "You look different."

I looked down at my outfit in confusion. "Umm, I'm the same me."

"Okay, Gretchen Jr.," he said with a grunt and brushed past me. I followed him to the living room.

Oh...he meant something else— or rather someone else.

"You want anything to drink or snack on?" I rocked on my heels, feeling nervous for some inexplicable reason. I guess because Daddy Randall had even more insight from God than my mama. He could always pull the truth from me with a simple look. Ever since I met him, he'd look at me, and I'd cave, telling him whatever he wanted to know which aggravated Gretchen. She tried to be all stubborn and hold out.

"I won't be here long. I just came to check in for a short time. Shavon is waiting on me at Talik's," he relayed and grunted as he sat down.

Randall Bennett was a nice looking, older man with little gray sprinkled between the hair on his head and face. I could see how Talik's mother, Ms. Shavon, was so taken with him. The man was suave and smooth like Billy Dee Williams in those movies my mama used make me watch with her.

He patted the cushion beside him. "Come sit and tell me about this man that has you grinning and blinding Heaven's angels with those pearly whites."

I laughed, trudging slowly to the sofa to sit beside the only earthly father figure I'd had in my life. "I can be grinning for a variety of reasons. A man is not the *only* reason for a woman's smile."

He gave me the look.

I spilled my guts, giddily sharing my feelings and telling him about how Victor made me feel. By the time I finished, I was breathing heavily like I'd run a race. I don't think I even took a breath during my confession.

Daddy Randall cocked his head to the side, a small smile curled up the left side of his mouth. "So, another funny man?"

I shrugged with a bashful grin.

"Figures since you and Gretchen love to giggle all the time. You know I'm going to check him out before I give my blessing."

"Of course you are," I retorted.

Internally, the little girl in me felt satisfyingly affirmed by Daddy Randall giving me the longed-for childhood experience of a father's response to his daughter dating a guy. Over the years, I dated but kept mum about the guy until he showed his true colors, and we went our separate ways. Marty was the first guy I'd introduced to Daddy Randall.

He did *not* approve of Marty.

"You kicked the Marty fellow and his meddlesome mama to the curb. Prayer definitely changes things," he joked with a big grin, and I laughed.

"You prayed for my relationship to fail, man?"

He looked at me aghast. "You didn't?"

I hollered. "I can't with you, Pastor."

We caught up for a few more minutes before he left to take his lil' boo out on a date. I closed the door behind him, thinking that Daddy Randall and Ms. Shavon had a more active dating life than me.

My thoughts turned to Victor as I went back to the living room to resume looking over the fabric samples for the athletic clothing line I wanted to present to Sherrie when she got back home. Victor and I were still taking baby steps towards getting to know one another. We were both busy individuals. Since the night I brought him leftovers from my mama, our growing relationship revolved around phone calls and texts. If he wasn't in meetings or out of town, I was in meetings or having to jump on a plane myself to meet up with fashion designers.

I wasn't complaining.

Nope.

Not at all.

I cherished whatever conversations Victor and I had, but I was thirsty for more. I wanted to spend quality time with him without our responsibilities intruding.

Just as I became engrossed in jotting down notes, someone knocked heavily on the door. I groaned at the intrusion before hopping up to see who had the nerve to come over unannounced.

More banging commenced. I yelled, "I'm coming! Hold your horses!"

I snatched the door open to find the man of my dreams looking devastatingly handsome with the biggest, most blinding smile on his face.

"Victor," I said on a soft sigh. My heart stuttered and tumbled in my chest. This man took my breath away.

He advanced on me, wrapping a muscled arm around my waist and pulled me into his arms before laying a swoon-worthy kiss on my lips.

Feeling lightheaded, I swayed back and forth with my eyes closed.

"Ah..." Victor hummed, nibbling on my lips. "Refreshing."

I blushed and sluggishly peeled my eyes open.

A satisfied smile awaited me. "I missed you, Filly."

I readily confessed, "I missed you too. Two weeks' worth of missing to be exact."

He laughed. "Two weeks, huh? I missed you two weeks and a day's worth."

Amused, I asked, "Are we going to be that couple? All disgustingly cute and stuff, trying to one-up one another."

He kissed me on the forehead before answering. "I refuse to be any other way. I wanna be Hello Kitty cute."

I threw my head back and laughed.

Victor moved back and stooped to retrieve a bag on the front porch. He held up the bag. "I brought food."

I ushered him in and quickly set up an eating area on the floor in the living room. Then, I helped him unpack the seafood pasta and garlic bread from their containers.

We kept relatively quiet as we ate. The only sounds in the room were silverware clanking against our plates and smacking. Sopping up the remaining sauce with his bread, he finally spoke as he pushed his empty plate across the table.

"That was good. Now, I need something sweet."

I sipped my water and joked, "You know...black people..." We both laughed.

"Tell me what I've missed in the life of the fashion guru since I've been gone."

Grinning at that, I told him, "I don't know about being a guru yet, but I've been unusually busy lately—"

"Which is a good thing."

"Yes, certainly a good thing. I just signed a contract for another black owned designer to have her new line in the store, and I've been working on my own line." I playfully bowed as he clapped. "Tell me about your jet-setting across the country, Mr. Comedian. I'm sure your expedition was way more exciting than mine."

He snorted. "If you think having to check people about calling me a trash, Black man who cheated on his wife and forced her to have an abortion is exciting."

"Do you want to talk about it?" I felt the waves of tension cloaked to his body. I saw the headline, and I wanted to find Tinashay and beat her behind. I could only imagine what he was feeling, especially after she confessed to him about having an abortion. And for her to turn around and fabricate this story that he forced her to have an abortion was downright evil.

Victor remained silent.

"We can talk about something else," I offered, touch his hand.

He shook his head and looked at me, his eyes conflicted. "I don't need to talk about my ex to you. I don't need her to come between us, to come between what we're building."

"She won't come between us unless we let her, Victor. This situation is clearly bothering you. I know it would bother me if it was me, and I am bothered to a certain extent because I can feel you."

"You can feel me?" An unreadable look crossed his face.

Feeling bold, I said, "I can feel you whenever you're in close proximity to me. Your joy, sadness, anger, grief— all of it is palpable. The first time we met, I felt the heaviness you carried in your heart. You smiled and laughed with the guys, but it was all an act. You were swimming in sorrow, and the get-together you forced yourself to attend was a lifeboat you needed to keep from going under."

He stared at me for a long time. I fought the urge to squirm under his stare. I couldn't shrink back because this was a defining moment in our budding romance.

Victor blinked as if coming out of a trance. Lifting my hand, he kissed it. "It wasn't just the get-together. It was you. I made eye contact with you, and something inside me shifted. God told me clear as day that everything was about to get better. Before I showed up to the party, I fought against going. I even started changing my clothes, but O knocked on the door and told me I needed to try. And I'm glad I did."

"I'm glad too." God moments never ceased to amaze me, and this one blew me away.

Victor opened up. "I'm so pissed off with Shay. It boggles my mind how she can do this to me. Keeping it one hundred, I asked God why. Why am I going through this after I've bent over backwards being the best husband I knew how to my wife?"

"I get it. When we don't understand what God is doing, we can fall into thinking that He's being silent and allowing us to suffer when really, He's aligning things in our favor."

Victor breathed in deeply. "Exactly how I feel. But I trust God. No matter how I feel or what happens, I gotta trust Him. It's hard though."

"It is hard, but you will make it through this test. People are waiting for you to break so they can replay your human moment on social media and write by-lines so they can say, 'See! I knew he wasn't a good guy.' I promise you I'm going to continue to intercede on your behalf because we will not let the enemy win."

Jerking me forward, his lips latched onto mine. He pulled away and ran his finger down my cheek. "Like I said earlier, you are refreshing, and I'm humbled it. Thank you."

We continued to catch up and share the details about our time apart. He helped me clean up the food and stash the leftovers in the kitchen. I showed him the fabric samples and my sketchbook filled with designs I wanted to mass reproduce.

"These are dope, Filly. You are so talented. I don't see how anyone can pass these up, and with so many people into fitness and health these days, I know they're going to sell."

"Thank you." I flushed, uncharacteristically pleased by his approval. "The plan before going full throttle in the marketplace is to get a few social media influencers to do reviews and give them affiliate codes for a test run."

"That's smart. I have a homeboy who owns a gym in L.A. He mostly sells unisex athletic wear in the gym and on his website. I can set up a meeting for you anytime you're ready."

"Really?" I got excited.

"I got you. Braeden loves to hype up Black entrepreneurs."

I know he ain't talking about who I think he's talking about. "Braeden?"

He looked at me like *duh, that's what I just said.* "Yeah, Braeden Harris."

"You know Braeden Harris? Wait one cotton-picking minute." I clutched his shirt in my fists, shaking him back and forth. "You're going to hook me up with Braedan Harris- AAAAAAAHHHHH!" Victor laughed as I shook him. I gasped, throwing my words together, "HESTHEMICHAELJORDANOFFITNESSANDIMGOINGTOWORKWITHHIM!!!!"

"Calm down, baby. I'm kinda jealous because you don't get this excited for me."

I snickered. "Yes, I do." I sobered once I thought about Tinashay using him for her career. I abhorred the thought of using him for his connections like she'd done. The possibility of working with Braedan Harris would be amazing, but I'd decline if it would remotely impact our relationship.

Frowning, he asked, "What's wrong?"

"I'm thinking about your history with your ex. I don't ever want to use you as a come up for my career."

Wrapping me up in his arms, Victor shushed me with a kiss. "You are not Shay. You are Athena Rose. My ex never worked hard for her connections. Everything she's ever accomplished is from her using me. I'm willingly offering to help you. You are tenacious and a hard worker. I see your work ethic, and I am going to help you. Case closed."

Get me together then, sir. "Okay, thank you, Victor Cole."

"You're welcome."

***

This was the most time we'd spent together.

I enjoyed every second of it and even told Victor what I was thinking.

"I like having you here. This is the first time we've spent together without social media or work interfering."

Shooting me a lazy smile and a wink from the other end of the sofa, he said, "We can have more days like this."

"How?"

"Melanie is back, and Sherrie will be back in a few days. I propose we take the next two weeks for us and really get to know one another. I've told Marianne to clear my schedule because I need to build this between us."

I thought about what he was asking. I had no meetings coming up. I did have vacation time, and I did deserve a break.

And I also wanted to be with him.

Being around him today unleashed a deep-seated yearning to be around him all the time. He'd hooked me.

While deep in thought, Victor had sat up and moved closer to me. "Think about it. We both have things going on, but I feel like this is the time for us to set the foundation for our future. I'll pay for your vacation days if I have to."

I smiled. "No need. I have the time."

"Check it. We can do whatever it is you want."

"What if I want to just laze around the house and occasionally go hiking or something else simple?" I just wanted to chill. Extravagance wasn't my forte. Extravagant clothes maybe, but not my extracurricular activities.

"Whatever you want," he promised. "I need this with you."

Stop making this man beg you. Say yes already.

"Let's do it," I agreed.

"Thank God! I was about to drop down on my knees."

I snickered at the relief on his face. You'd think I was the celebrity, and he was the average Joe who was trying to impress me. He didn't know I was already impressed with him, celebrity or not.

Victor was way more intentional than Marty. He fed me, showered me with genuine compliments, and affirmed my career aspirations. He never made me feel as if I had to second guess myself around him.

"You know the guys around here have done this sort of thing for my girls."

He nodded. "I know. I got the idea from Owen and Talik. Owen said he took Sherrie on a month-long vacation, and they came back married."

"They did, and Talik spent two weeks with Mel doing dangerous activities like skydiving. I'm good on that."

"Girl, me too. I'm not trying to die any time soon."

"We need to set the ground rules."

"Like what?"

"No social media."

"Done. No canceling dates unless you're dying."

I sputtered laughing. "What? Never mind." I shook my head. "I won't cancel dates unless I'm dying. Same goes for you, sir. Double dates? My girls are going to wanna see us together."

"Agreed, but they cannot monopolize all of our time. They get three hours at the most."

"I concur. Any disagreements, we resolve them on the spot."

"Most definitely, and we make up with my lips on yours." He grinned mischievously.

I blushed. "Which brings me to another one. No playing hide the pickle."

Victor's face balled up in confusion. "Hide the pickle? What kind of backwoods stuff is that?"

Laughing, I said, "You know what I mean. No sex."

"Oh, say that next time with your country self. Hide the pickle," he mumbled, shaking his head at me. I laughed at him. "No sex. I can do that as long as you keep your hands to yourself. All of this chocolate is tempting."

I rolled my eyes with a grin. "I can keep my hands to myself."

"Any more rules?"

"Nope."

It was settled. I was about to get quality time.

Ch. 10

Victor

"Welcome home." I said, extending my arm to invite Athena into my new home, which I closed on a few days ago.

"Don't you mean welcome to my home?" she asked, brushing past me.

"That's what I said," I murmured as I admired her in the sundress that matched the color of her skin while she inspected the foyer of the house.

Athena was stunning.

Inside and out.

With her inner matching her outer, I was hard-pressed not to stare at her like a weirdo. *Today, though...geez...I'm a weirdo.* I couldn't help but stare. Her sun kissed skin glimmered in the sunlight filtering through the transom windows.

And she smelled delicious.

Down boy.

Shaking myself out of my Athena trance, I watched her twirl around, amused at my response.

"That is not what you said. This is not my home. It's yours, so you should say, and I quote, 'Welcome to my home, Athena.' See how I did that?"

I pretended to play along. "Welcome home, Athena."

Throwing her head back, she laughed, exposing the alluring column of her slender neck, and I immediately transformed back into the weirdo.

I slid my hands into my pockets to temper the wild impulse to snatch her up and devour her. Nah, I couldn't do that because I definitely wouldn't be able to stop.

It would be best to keep my hands to myself for now until I got myself under control.

***

Athena

"I want to help. Why do you keep moving away from me? I don't bite."

I could've sworn he said, "Yeah, but I do."

"What was that?" I watched Victor swallow thickly and nervously move around the kitchen as he clumsily gathered the ingredients for our dinner.

I'd never seen Victor Cole nervous. Suave and cool with a side of goofiness, yes, but this nervous energy emanating from him was new but actually endearing and adorable.

He'd yet to kiss me. The other day when he showed up, he was so touchy-feely. But today, he was doing everything to avoid me.

I wanted my hug.

And I wanted my kiss, darn it!

"I said you don't have to do anything because I got it." He answered with his back to me.

Umm hmm.

I was about to take my hug and kiss by force because he was playing with me. *Don't get me all hype and addicted to your hugs and kisses and then deprive me.*

I eased up behind him and wrapped my arms around his waist. His body stiffened, and he let out the most tortured groan.

I instantly let him go, thinking maybe he was hurt, and I exasperated his injury.

"I'm so sorry. Where are you hurt?" I asked, turning him around.

His eyes looked pained as he grunted, "I tried to be good."

"What—"

His lips cut me off.

***

Victor

My little filly unleashed the beast earlier. We both had self-control, thank God. After teasing me for running from her, we put our hormones on ice and commenced cooking together, eating together, and then cleaning up together.

We then retired to the sofa, hugged up and laughing about any and everything.

The act was so domestic. I realized how much I missed engaging in domesticity. Doing it with Athena more than made up for the loss of it in my failed marriage.

I didn't want to let her go back home.

I was so close to asking her to move in for the next two weeks.

However, I knew that was asking for trouble.

***

Athena

"Come on, old man!" I hollered at Victor several yards behind me.

"Remind me...to...get...you back...woo," he wheezed, leaning to the side.

He was so funny.

I teased, "What happened to being in better shape than me, sir?"

He grinned, wiping the sweat from his face. "I'm just getting warmed up."

I was too tickled. He bet me that he'd be able to out hike me on *my* hiking trail. I was an expert when it came to Copeland's trails. But his machismo convinced him he could beat me.

Pffttt...men.

"Yeah, okay because you huffing and puffing and about to blow your kneecaps out just says that you are getting your second wind." He glared at me, and I cackled loudly. "Come on," I said in a baby voice and patted my thighs as if encouraging a little kid. "You can do it, little Victor. There you go. One foot in front of the other."

Victor was glaring at me and making progress to get closer to me. A couple more steps and he'd be upon me.

"Ohhhh," I drawled out. "That's a good boy! I—"

This fool tackled me, pinning me down to the ground.

I laughed so hard. "Victor, let me up."

"Nope." He bit my earlobe, making me squeal. "You shouldn't have messed with me."

I growled, "You are getting my hair dirty. Always wanting to tussle with me."

"It's fake anyway."

I busted out laughing. "No, you didn't! Get off me." I bucked against his big body. The action didn't move him at all.

"Apologize, and I'll let you go."

I stared into his handsome face, realizing how happy I was. My heart felt like it was going to burst open and gush out heart emojis. That's how happy I was.

He was happy too. I felt how light his spirit was.

"Are you going to apologize today or tomorrow?"

"I'll apologize on one condition." Easing my hand up, I moved it towards the target.

"What's that?" Thinking he had the upper hand, his body relaxed.

Very demurely, I asked, "If you give me a kiss, I'll say sorry."

"Rewarding your bad behavior," he scoffed, grinning down at me. "I don't think so."

Batting my eyes at him, I begged, "Please, baby."

His eyes softened. *Got him.* "This kiss is for me, not you."

"Okay." My voice was deceptively soft.

As soon as his lips touched mine, I pounced, putting pressure on his hip bone. He was ticklish there. He confessed that was one of his weaknesses the other day, and I'm sure he never thought it would be used against him so soon.

"Agghhhh! Girl!"

Laughing, I pushed him off me and jumped up in victory to crow, "All I do is win, old man."

Spry as his alter ego, Black Ninja, he jumped to his feet and chased me.

We frolicked in the woods for another hour like some little kids, tiring one another out.

We were going to sleep good tonight.

***

Victor

"The separation was the final nail in the coffin. Not the infidelity. Not the constant emasculation. I was willing to put up with her mess because I believed in the marriage. Was I perfect? No because I have my ways too, but I believed in us. It took her filing for a divorce for me to wake the hell up. It hurt, and I even shed some tears, but God gave me the wakeup call I needed to let go of a marriage I realized this past year shouldn't have ever happened. You know some men wouldn't even think about staying in a relationship after a woman cheats, but I did."

Athena's understanding eyes met mine, her soft hand stroking my beard. "You fought for your marriage. I think that's commendable. Sometimes, one partner can see when the end is right in front of their faces and should end things the right way but take the coward's way out by pushing people away. Meanwhile, the other partner feigns ignorance because of familiarity and comfort. This partner refuses to add more hurt on top of the hurt the relationship has endured since everything seems to be all good as it coasts on top of unaddressed problems. So, effort to not rock the boat takes precedence."

"Are you talking about the Martian?" She yanked my beard, and I chuckled.

"Yes, I'm talking about Marty. He was the one who ended things, and I tried to stay around because he was comfortable. He checked the preconceived boxes for the appropriate mate. The red flags were there, but I wanted the ring."

I grunted.

She yanked my beard again, laughing. "Thank God, Marty and Tinashay did what we couldn't do on our own."

The thought of missing out on this made my stomach hurt.

The way this woman had me moving and feeling all clingy, I knew she was my true rib.

She occupied my mind all day. I wondered what she was doing when we were apart. I hated to leave her for a second and counted down the time until I could be around her.

These past few days of nonstop Athena Nakoma Rose dispelled all thoughts of the world outside of our little cocoon.

I was in love.

***

Athena

Laying in the hammock Victor put up for me in his huge backyard, we cuddled under the shade trees in bliss.

"I want to travel the world with you. I'm afraid to fly even though I've been to Paris before and have to fly on occasion for work, but I know with you I'll fight my fears to experience the joys of travelling and making forever memories."

I couldn't believe what I just said. How did he pull these confessions out of me?

Tilting my chin up, he stared down into my eyes. "Let's do it. We can hop on a plane today and go wherever you want."

Was he serious? "Seriously?"

"You can get whatever you want from me." Yeah, he was serious.

"But how can you charter a flight last minute? Won't we have to wait?"

He pinched my lips closed. "Let your man worry about that. I got you."

I hesitated a second before saying, "Okay."

"Now, tell me where you want to go."

***

"Mr. Cole, we are preparing for takeoff."

Victor thanked the flight attendant. He turned to me and buckled me in. "You ready?"

Anxiety and excitement created a cacophony of emotions. I jerkily nodded and pressed my back to the seat, letting my eyes slam close.

This is crazy.

Victor really chartered a last-minute flight to Saint Lucia.

His deep voice filtered into my ear as he murmured, "Hold my hand, baby. I'm not going anywhere because we're in this together."

My eyes popped open. Our eyes met and held, and I saw the forever memories in the depths of his eyes. He was never more beautiful to me at that moment.

"Tell me what you see," Victor commanded.

"I see...I see forever."

My heart and the plane took off together.

I clenched Victor's hand while maintaining eye contact.

"Me too, Filly."

Ch. 11

Athena

Encased in the arms of the man, who I was wide open for, and watching the sunset on the balcony of our island villa with an ocean view was everything.

Everything.

This moment couldn't get any better.

"Athena?"

"Hmmm."

"Look at me."

I lazily turned to give my man my undivided attention.

"I'm in love with you."

My eyes watered at how self-assured he looked. I believed him because I felt his love.

Throwing caution to the wind, I responded with the same confidence, "I'm in love with you too."

This moment actually did get better.

***

"We all have our own history with God, whether we know He exists or worship Him because He exists or even if some chooses to deny His existence— the history is there. But relationship is on the opposite end of the spectrum. When did you fall in love with God?"

I propped my elbows up on the elegantly set table, leaning in to hear his answer.

Tattoos gleaming in the soft light, I smiled at the handsome vision before me.

Victor's full lips spread into a nostalgic smile. "That's a good question. I fell in love with God when I totally surrendered my will and my way for His. As I grasped how much God really loves me and wants the best for me after I've been dismissive of Him and separated myself because I wanted to do my own thing, I fell for Him. No one can do me better than God. Not even myself because I don't always make the best decisions for myself. After everything I've done in absence of Him, God still welcomes me with open arms and loves me for me."

"I love that," I responded with a grin.

He filled his mouth with seafood risotto, chewed, and swallowed before asking the same of me. I swallowed the bite of the braised short rib Victor ordered for me before answering.

"Basically, for the same reasons you just said, but it was in those moments when I questioned my worthiness because I didn't have a father around. I wanted a father so bad. Daddy Randall was a good fill-in at times, but I wanted my own father. I used to cry myself to sleep, asking God why I had to be fatherless. And you know what happened?"

"What?"

"While I slept, I would dream about having a father. This nameless and faceless man, who I knew with every fiber of my being was my daddy, would take me to get ice cream, to the park, to the movies, and on daddy-daughter dates. I would wake up the next morning feeling refreshed and so loved. My feelings from the previous day were absent. I later realized when I got older that God relieved the void I felt from not having a present father by visiting me in my dreams. Sometimes, I get chill bumps from thinking about it." I shivered, growing misty. "I know He loves me, so I choose to love Him in return."

"Who wouldn't serve a God like that?" Victor raised his glass, and I raised mine.

Clink, clink.

"Who wouldn't indeed."

***

Victor

"Hey lady!" I greeted my mom via FaceTime.

"Hey, my baby. How are you?"

"I'm good. Enjoying my downtime. I decided to get away from my getaway."

"Oh, really? Where are you?" Mom's excitement was so adorable.

"St. Lucia."

"Well, you look rested and happy. Last time I saw you, you were tense and so stern, but you look like you've laid all your burdens down. *Burdens down, Lord.... Burdens down, Lord....*"

I shook my head at my Mom breaking into song. Athena giggled, and I winked at her. She was patiently waiting for me to bring her into the frame.

Mom stopped singing and peered at the phone. Just nosy. "Who are you winking at?"

"Come here." I pulled a suddenly bashful Athena into view. "This is Athena... my girlfriend."

"Oh, sweet Jesus! You are so beautiful. Hey, darling." She waved at the screen.

Athena grinned. "Hi, Mrs. Cole."

"Victor, she's a doll."

"Thank you." Athena blushed.

"Her hair is fake though, but I don't mind."

Mom gasped, and Athena laughed as she punched me, making me laugh. The phone jostled, and I quickly righted it before it could fall out of my hands.

"That's right, baby. Beat his behind," my mom trilled.

"I'm just playing," I said, kissing Athena on the underside of her ear. "You know you're my baby."

"Tell that to my hair," she said with a pout.

I grabbed a fistful of her extensions, whispering, "I'm sorry bundles."

We shared a laugh.

"Y'all are too cute." Mom beamed, then yelled for my dad. "William! Come here! Your son is on the phone with our new daughter-in-law."

Me and Athena shared a look.

"Who Victor?"

Seconds later, William Cole's face filled the screen.

"Well, how you doing, young lady?" Dad asked with a pleased grin. I knew what he was thinking. He approved.

"I'm good. How are you, Mr. Cole?"

"Happy to know my boy is smiling again."

The call continued until plans were made for them to meet Athena in person soon. I called my bro and Faith next, and they gushed over Athena as well. It felt good to see her interact with my family unguarded.

***

Athena

"Where are you?" Gretchen asked by way of hello.

I laughed at her. "Where I'm at."

"Don't sass me, young lady," she fussed, sounding like my mama.

"I'm in St. Lucia. Have been for the past four days."

The line quieted.

"Hello?" I pulled the phone back to see if she was still on the line.

"Quit playing. Where are you, for real?"

I put the call on speaker and went to our text thread to send pictures to her. "I'm in St. Lucia. Check your text messages. I just sent you proof."

She gasped. "You're really on an island with your man. Y'all just up and left and won't even answer y'all's phones. We thought someone had kidnapped y'all."

"My bad. It was a spur-of-the-moment, and we've been—"

"All up each other's behinds and forgot about your friends."

I snickered. "I plead the fifth."

"I understand. Otis had me wide open and doing things on the fly too, so I get it. These pictures are too cute. Y'all look so good together, and I can tell you two are deeply infatuated."

"He told me he loved me."

"Bestie, I know he turned you into mush."

I grinned, remembering that moment on this same balcony. "He did. It was so romantic, Gretch. The sun was setting, and I was wrapped in his arms. The whole day was amazing, really. We took a helicopter tour of the island, then had a couple's massage at the spa. We had lunch on the beach, and then we hit the open market. He wanted to buy everything I touched."

"Please tell me you let the man spoil you."

"At first, I didn't, but he wore me down." I looked down, admiring the turquoise bracelet on my wrist. Victor chose it and several other pieces of jewelry for me.

"I'm so happy for you, best friend. You deserve this, and I'm glad it's Victor. Apparently, he's the right man for the job."

I sighed, feeling so at peace. "Gretch, I love this man so much. He's intentional and so forthcoming about himself. He doesn't hold back, and that facilitates my own openness with him. I feel safe. Outside of God, Victor is my safe place. That scares me and excites me."

"Lean on the excitement because fear will try to talk you out of your blessing."

I said, "Oh, I know. I'm too far gone to turn back now. Victor Cole has my heart."

"And you have mine."

Phone in hand, I turned and smiled at how handsome he looked in his white linen outfit.

"Marty could never!" Gretchen hollered.

He and I laughed at her shenanigans.

"We have to get going, Gretchen," Victor told her. "We have dinner plans."

"I'm glad you are alive and not being held hostage. Have fun and send me more pictures."

"Will do. Love you, Gretch."

"Love you too."

Ending the call, I took Victor's outstretched hand.

***

Victor

I could get used to this.

Her soft snores and relaxed face while sleeping in my arms produced a deep yearning for us to be like this all the time.

I asked for one night in my arms. I just wanted one night together. Last night, for some reason, I couldn't spend away from her. She hesitated, then acquiesced after I promised that I'd keep us both accountable.

I looked down into her beautiful face, knowing this woman had my heart.

I was prepared to be alone for a long time after my divorce, but God had other plans.

"I love you," I whispered and kissed her on the lips.

Her eyes fluttered then opened. A smile peeped out once she realized I was staring at her. "Good morning."

"Good morning."

"What time is it?"

"Almost noon."

Her eyes widened. "Wow, I never sleep this late."

"Me neither. I just woke up a few minutes ago."

She stretched and resettled in my arms. "We're playing a dangerous game."

"I know."

This feeling was addictive, but I couldn't help myself.

"I'm getting addicted to you."

"Is that a bad thing?"

"Not unless you don't feel the same way. Good thing I *know* you feel the same way."

***

Athena

"Goodbye, St. Lucia." I poked out my bottom lip. Staring out of the jet's window, I wished we didn't have to leave.

"I promise we'll be back. Okay?"

"Okay."

It was time to go back home. Pretty soon, our two-week sabbatical would be over, and we'd be back in the real world.

I wondered what awaited us.

Ch. 12

Athena

Flashing lights momentarily blinded me, causing me to drop Victor's hand to cover my eyes. Looking from under the shadow of my hand, I strained my eyes to find Victor beside me. Panic began to set in when my vision remained blurry, and I flailed my hand around, trying to find him.

A crowd of aggressive and invasive voices suddenly surrounded us.

"Victor, is Athena who you cheated on your wife with?"

Cheated with me? What!?

"Victor, did you really make your wife have an abortion because Athena is pregnant?"

Pregnant? These people were crazy.

"Did you elope in St. Lucia?"

NO!

"How far along are you, Athena?"

This is crazy...

"How long were you having an affair?"

"Do you care that Tinashay tried to commit suicide?"

Wait...what?

Tinashay tried to commit suicide? When?

I felt sick to my stomach at the questions yelled our way. They knew my name. Possibly knew where I lived and where I worked.

How did they know we were gone?

How did they know when we were landing?

"I got you." The calm in Victor's voice somewhat calmed me as he grabbed my hand and plowed through the crowd of paparazzi.

I was in a near sprint, trying to keep up with Victor's long legs. The two airport security officers finally noticed what was going on, and thankfully, rushed to our rescue and headed the crowd off, allowing us to escape to the waiting SUV. Victor quickly threw our bags into the back.

Diving into the backseat, I tried to combat the anxiety of what just happened.

"This is a private airport. Why in the world did Luther allow them on his property?" the driver asked, looking at us through the rearview mirror.

Victor answered because I was clueless and still agitated. "They always find a way, my man. Always."

"Couldn't be me."

Secretly, I felt the same way.

I couldn't handle this, could I? Victor seemed indifferent by what just happened back there, and here I was trying not to have a total meltdown.

Victor grabbed his phone and turned off the do not disturb. Notifications rolled in. He quickly swiped the deluge and made a phone call.

Those questions were embarrassing and insulting. I was innocent. People were going to hate me. They were going to castigate and eviscerate me in the blogs. I'd have to delete my social media accounts—that's if...No, no, they had to have already combed through my accounts already.

My privacy was officially gone.

You're dating a celebrity. What did you think was going to happen?

Was I really that naïve?

Apparently so because I was so in love that I forgot Victor was a celebrity. He wasn't a celebrity when we were together. I only saw him, the man.

But this...

This was too much.

"Athena, hey," Victor cautiously called. "Are you okay?"

Unable to verbalize my feelings, I shook my head, tears filling my eyes. They spilled over as Victor grabbed me. I fell into his arms and cried.

"I'm sorry. I should've had the forethought to have additional security around. The first time is always jarring, but I think—"

"I can't do this!" I jerked away and wiped the still spilling tears from my face.

Victor looked so crestfallen that I cried harder.

"What are you saying, Filly?"

What was I saying? I loved Victor and could see him as my husband and the father of my kids. But this drama was way beyond my purview. I questioned if our love could sustain his celebrity? Him and Tinashay didn't make it, and they had years together.

Why would we be any different?

"This is scary," I cried, voice cracking.

"Baby," Victor implored with an earnest expression, "don't give up on me, please."

I broke down crying again, feeling horrible. This man had made himself vulnerable to me on multiple occasions, and here I was deflecting soon as a problem arose.

He pulled me into his arms and whispered how much he loved me and that we could weather any storm because we were meant to be.

Twenty minutes later, Victor helped me bring my luggage and souvenirs into the house. I walked the short distance to my room and deposited my things next to the bed. I needed a minute to get myself together, so I went into the bathroom. The vision of my splotchy face saddened me.

I turned on the water and quickly washed my face, then moisturized.

I made up my mind after rechecking my appearance.

Victor was my forever, and I wouldn't kick him to the curb because of people who didn't matter. Our love was worth fighting for.

I left out of the bathroom and pulled up at the sight of Victor sitting on the side of my bed. His face was miserable.

"Are we going to be okay?"

"We are."

Relief covered his face.

"I've had my head in the clouds, and I failed to think about how our lives, my life, would be impacted by yours. I...cracked under pressure because of that, and I'm sorry for doing so. I know what we have is real. It's just that I have to factor in reality."

"Being in the clouds isn't necessarily a bad thing, but I get what you're saying. I'm just as guilty about being a space cadet." He smiled.

I giggled and sniffled.

"Now that we know this area of weakness, it's up to us to make sure we got us."

I nodded, moving towards him. "God got us, and we got us."

He pulled me into him, causing me to straddle his lap. Nose to nose, we breathed in one another. He exhaled, and I inhaled.

Another strand added to the cord, further strengthening our bond.

"Thank you for not giving up on me."

"Thank you for believing in us."

I felt even better when he told me that there was no suicide attempt. Someone started the rumor online. Tinashay dispelled the rumor by going live and reassuring her fans.

I guess that's one good thing she did.

***

"Look at 'em, Legs!" Otis said that so loud that Victor and I stopped walking to look down at ourselves.

When I looked back up, the whole gang was facing us with their arms folded. Victor and I shared an amused glance. Gretchen stood back, grinning from ear to ear.

"Looking all moisturized and *happy*," Otis snapped, making us laugh. He frowned. "Ain't nothing funny. How y'all just gone come up missing and not answer the phone?"

"Then have the nerve to walk in here casually holding hands like we almost didn't file a missing person's report, huh bae?" Gretchen instigated with a cheshire grin.

My narrowed gaze at her promised retribution. She only grinned harder.

I know we proposed no phones during our getting-to-know-you honeymoon, but we couldn't not communicate with our people. I let Gretchen know before we unintentionally went dark in St. Lucia that my communication would be inconsistent, but I would try to respond daily just to check-in during our seclusion here in Copeland. But I guess the four days Victor and I were so wrapped up in one another, we lost track of time and a bit of reality.

"Athena Rose, I know good and well you didn't run off and let this handsome thing impregnate you—gosh you're handsome! Never mind, my grandbaby is going to be gorgeous."

I jumped back. My mama materialized out of nowhere. But there she was in the flesh, looking up at Victor with heart eyes. Everybody in the backyard laughed, including Victor.

"Ma, I'm not pregnant."

She waved me off. "That's alright. You can always try next time."

I sputtered out, "I know my Christian mama is not okay with me getting pregnant out of wedlock?"

She pursed her lips at me and frowned. "Of course I don't condone it, guh. I'm saying next time it will be because the marriage bed will be undefiled. Hint, hint." She smiled at Victor, who grinned.

"Ms. Rose, it's nice to finally meet you." Victor swooped her up into a hug and kissed her cheek.

"Call me mama."

No subtlety at all. I shook my head, following dutifully behind Victor and my gushing mama.

We spent the evening catching up with our friends and my mama. The atmosphere was light and carefree, even though outside of our bubble people were going berserk with innuendos and accusations about me being a homewrecker and all types of other craziness.

Yesterday's ambush knocked me temporarily off my game, but my head was back on straight.

I looked across Gretchen and Otis's backyard, catching Victor's eye. He winked, and I smiled.

We were good.

***

A knock at the door pulled me from my brainstorming. I hated being interrupted during my thinking process when I was designing. Victor knew this. That's why I gave him a key last week before we left for St. Lucia.

"Victor, why didn't you use your key?" I huffed, walking to the door. Checking my attitude, I remembered he went to get groceries. Maybe his hands were full.

I opened the door to find Marty standing there.

And he was steaming mad.

At me.

And for what?

"What's your malfunction?" I asked, wondering why he was at my door.

"Mother was right."

I scoffed at his self-righteous tone. "Be for real, Marty. You think your mother is always right about everything."

He smirked. "She was right about you, you floozy."

My mouth gaped. "What did you call me?"

"I called you the floozy that you are. Mother said you were probably cheating on me, and you proved it by cavorting around town with Victor Cole. I knew something was going on last summer when he couldn't keep his beady little eyes off you."

What grown, Black man talked like that? It was ridiculous, and his ridiculousness was making me mad.

"First, if you're going to insult me, how about using a term that's not from the fifties," I heavily emphasized with sarcasm. "This is what I'm going to do, Marty. I'm going to give you one chance to leave right now. No hard feelings." I was hot but kept my composure.

I looked him over, wondering what I ever saw in him. Marty wasn't a bad looking guy, and he was sweet to a fault, well…was sweet.

If you looked close enough, you could actually see how spineless he actually was (excluding his spark of courage right now).

"I'm glad I broke up with you, and I'm glad I told the media what a conniving floozy you really were."

Time out! "You did what?"

I advanced on him so fast. Grabbing him by his meticulously pressed, tucked in shirt, I yoked him up and was about to toss him off the porch until Victor showed up.

"Filly, let him go," Victor pleaded with mirth shining from his eyes, trying to pry my fingers off Marty's shirt.

I wanted to shake him like a ragdoll.

"Fine!" I said, letting it go. "Get off my porch, Marty, and don't come back because if you do, I'm going to beat you're a—whew!" I caught myself and pointed. "Just go."

His face was red with embarrassment. Unsuccessfully trying to smooth his wrinkled shirt, Marty backed away and gave one last parting shot. "You're not worth it anyway."

Victor moved in front of me to face Marty. "Alright, you better go before I let Filly finish you off."

I couldn't help laughing, which infuriated Marty. Victor was so unserious sometimes.

We watched Marty screech off in his Ford Focus.

Victor howled laughing.

"What?" I slapped his arm.

"I can't believe you messed with a dude who drives a Ford Focus."

I pushed him in the chest. "Shut up."

Ch. 13

Victor

I hated doing damage control.

The blogs weren't letting up on me or Athena.

I was proud of my baby. She was taking it all in stride, and that blip from the airport a few days ago caused some friction, but we were stronger for it.

Today was our last day of seclusion, but I had to take this meeting with the CEO of MelanTech, the black-owned jewelry company who chose me to endorse their watches.

They initially pushed for an in-person meeting, however, they conceded to a virtual meeting at Marianna's request.

I refused to leave Athena on our last day.

"Vic, you promised that you had things under control with this narrative concerning your personal life," Taheem said, brushing his locs out of his face.

"We're working on it. Victor Cole is the same man who endorsed you in the infancy of your company, Taheem. When no other celebrity would collaborate with you, Victor did. He's been your biggest mouthpiece, biggest client, and biggest supporter. Let's not forget those facts because his ex-wife and the media want to create salacious headlines and damage my client's reputation."

Marianna to the rescue.

Taheem looked away from the camera. He silently conferred with his partner, Rocko.

The possibility of losing one of my favorite endorsements upset me. This was business, and I understood their stance. Bad press could cripple their company, but at the same time, I was a big supporter of MelanTech. For them to question my loyalty because of headlines frustrated me.

Rocko spoke up. "Vic, man I have love for you, and I do appreciate everything you've done for this company. Man to man. Not your publicist. I want to hear your side of the story."

Marianna frowned at the request. I signaled to her that it was cool.

"I'm not a cheater. Have never cheated and will never cheat. Shay asked for a divorce last year after all avenues of avoiding a separation were exhausted. I wanted kids. They didn't happen, and I took that as God's will. I also accepted the demise of my marriage as God's will. The breakdown set me up to meet the love of my life." Rocko smiled, and him and Taheem simultaneously nodded in understanding. "Y'all know I'm a man of faith. I'm not about mudslinging and pointing fingers to cast blame, but I am a man who knows when playing the long game of patience and silence will pay off in time. I appreciate the working relationship we built, but I understand if you need to break ties. I know this is business and not personal."

"No, man. We love working with you too," Taheem refuted.

Rocko chimed in, "I agree. We just needed something from you because you hadn't said anything."

"So, gentleman," Marianna slid back into the conversation, "my client's contract is no longer in jeopardy."

"We're good," Rocko confirmed.

Crisis averted.

We talked for another half hour. Rocko presented a new line they were working on just with me in mind. I felt relieved knowing they actually did not want to cancel our contract.

"Okay, boss. I need to get back to it. I'll talk to you tomorrow. You have a few meetings to attend tomorrow. You gotta hit the ground running because the time away with your amore has us behind schedule."

Giving her a disbelieving glare, I asked, "Behind schedule, Marianna?"

She laughed. "Not really behind schedule."

"You really mean behind your schedule. Relax because I'm not rushing anything."

She groaned. "I don't know how to relax. I am glad you are learning to." She smiled softly. "Love looks good on you. I heard what you didn't say about Athena when you told Rocko and Taheem that you met the love of your life."

"I can't lie. This is the best I felt in a long time. Athena is everything."

"She has to be to get you smiling the way you are right now."

I laughed. "Man, whatever. I'll talk to you tomorrow."

"Will do, jefe. Tell Athena I said hello."

I ended the video feed, and Athena rounded the corner.

"Finally!" She bounced towards the sofa and sat on my lap. "I'm ready for my crochet lesson. I need to let off some steam."

Though she teased me previously (and still did) about crocheting, she asked me to show her how to crochet something simple.

The lessons were funny as heck. My baby was so uncoordinated.

***

"How is it that I can design bomb clothes and co-ordinate a bomb outfit but can't crochet to save my life?" Athena chunked the crochet hook and thread across the room.

I calmly responded as I continued to make the small, receiving blanket for my future niece or nephew "Not everyone can be me."

She cut her eyes at me, and I laughed.

Placing my materials on the table in front of me, I pulled pouting Athena into my arms. "I'm sorry," I placated, kissing and nipping her jaw.

"I give up. Crocheting is not my ministry. Guess I'll stick to what I know best."

"I agree."

I laughed as she swung on me. I jumped up in just enough time to avoid the blow. Not to be deterred, she grabbed one of the decorative pillows on the sofa and chased me around the house.

Eventually, I let her catch me.

***

After the crocheting lesson, I suggested we take a ride somewhere.

Riding around Copeland was relaxing. The radio serenaded us as we laughed and talked about different things.

On the way back to my house, we stopped at the restaurant to get burgers and fries.

"I'm glad I didn't listen to you…talking about get you one burger. You know you like to eat." She'd demolished one burger already before we made it back home. I lived like seven minutes away from the restaurant.

"Oh, be quiet. You don't know me."

I grinned. "Girl, I do know you. That's why I bought you two burgers."

"I like to eat," she said, munching on her fries.

"I know," I emphasized.

She laughed. "Whatever, Victor."

"I like that you eat like a grown man."

Athena tried to punch me. I intercepted and took a big bite of her hand, making her squeal. I kissed the bite mark and basked in her signature scent of coconut and vanilla. I couldn't get enough of her smell.

I cruised into my neighborhood. Our lighthearted banter halted at the unidentified vehicle parked in my circular driveway. Someone was sitting in the car. I couldn't make out who it was from behind.

"Expecting company?" Athena asked, looking over the Mercedes.

"Nah, not on our last day together. I told everyone to stay away."

I exited and rounded the vehicle to help Athena step down. Whoever it was, opened the car as soon as I closed the door behind Athena.

My mouth went slack when I realized it was Shay.

"Surprise!"

I swore I felt steam billowing from my ears. I worked on my anger daily, but Shay showing up here was not a good look.

"Surprise, surprise, indeed," Athena gritted out.

Lord, get your daughter.

***

Athena departed with our bags of food and a, "Do what needs to be done," and went in the house, leaving me outside to deal with Shay.

"Shay, why?" I was vexed by her appearance.

"The better question is why her and not me?"

My face twisted up so fast. "Maybe I missed the signs because clearly something is mentally challenging you. I mean, it'll explain your behavior. To be honest, I'm relieved that I finally know the cause of the accusations."

Stomping her stiletto encased foot, she demanded, "Who is she!?"

Okay, bro, you can't reason with crazy. "Shay go back to Cali where you belong. I can't do this— no, I won't do this. You divorced me. I've accepted it, and I've moved on."

"Do you love her?" Shay stared at the house.

I started to ignore the question, but only the truth worked with Shay. "Yes, I'm in love with her."

She jerked back as if I hit her. Shaking her head wildly, she mumbled, "No."

"No?" What did she mean by *no*?

"I don't accept this. I know you still love me." She rushed me, trying to wrap her arms around me.

"Shay, get off me, for real!" I tried to push her back. They said crazy people had crazy strength. Shay made a firm believer out of me today.

"I called the police," Athena said, hurrying out of the house. Shay let me go and rounded on Athena.

"HE DOESN'T LOVE YOU!" Shay screamed in her face.

Lord, for real, please get your daughter.

"This isn't over," Shay vowed, running to her car and burning rubber out of my driveway.

My life was turning into a Tubi movie on steroids.

"I think you should get a restraining order." I heard the alarm in Athena's voice.

I was equally alarmed.

***

O clowned me for the first five minutes of our conversation, but he did agree that I needed a restraining order.

"Bruh, protect yourself and Athena. Do not stop. Do not pass go and collect two hundred dollars. Get to the police station and file first thing Monday morning because chicks like that are diabolical. Protect yourself man. God told you not to retaliate. He never said not to protect yourself."

I signed, running a hand over my head. "This is crazy man. I've never seen Shay unhinged like that. Now, I have to worry about Athena. She got quiet after the whole scene in front of the house. She said she needed a minute."

"Give her minute. Let her process everything. Legs is on the phone with her now trying to talk her out of going Mighty Morphin Power Rangers on Shay."

I laughed. "Be serious."

He chuckled. "I am serious right now. Sis is hot right now. Like I said, just chill out. Athena loves you, and believe me, she ain't going anywhere."

I felt reassured that today wasn't like the airport.

"Man, go do your Yoda thing. Pray and read some scriptures."

Get some friends in comedy, they say. I shook my head, laughing. I wouldn't trade my boy for nothing.

Ending the call, I went to have me a talk with Jesus.

Afterwards, I called Marianna to inform her of what happened.

I texted O right quick. I needed him to go with me somewhere tomorrow.

Plan in place, I went to bed wishing Athena was next to me.

Ch. 14

Athena

Gretchen had me messed up right now. Gone ask if I felt threatened by Tinashay.

Girl, bye.

"No, I'm not threatened by Tinashay. Not today, not yesterday, not ever. She ain't no better than me." My neck was swinging, and my finger was waving.

"She has more money."

Mel and Sherrie snickered.

"Gretch, don't make me snatch you."

She left her desk and hugged me. I shrugged her off. "Leave me alone, traitor."

"Aww, don't be like that bestie."

I laughed as I dodged her. "You're just as childish as your husband."

Sherrie, the calm one in our rambunctious group, asked, "On a serious note, how are you holding up with the scrutiny and dealing with Tinashay?"

Closing my sketchbook, I thought about it. More paparazzi showed up this morning at the shop ever since Tinashay let it be known she was in Copeland to get her husband back (the police were called). Social media was engaged, awaiting with bated breath any new information about our supposed love triangle.

I wasn't tripping about it because I knew Victor's heart— even though I hadn't heard from him since yesterday. I asked him for a minute, and I know he took it literally. A minute for me meant a couple hours at the most.

"I'm aggravated. People say the dumbest, most vile stuff on social media like they have firsthand knowledge of our lives. It's so annoying. I had to turn the comments off to get peace because people bought some audacity and had the nerve to actually use it by telling me what I should and shouldn't be doing."

Mel shot a sympathetic smile my way. "Internet trolls are the worst. A simple post of someone having coffee turns into a debate and name-calling. It's ridiculous."

"Gretchen, when you went through it, you seemed so unfazed." I remembered when her and Otis's elopement went viral. Many were unkind until Otis went LIVE and let it be known he wasn't about to allow them to bother his wife.

Gretchen volleyed her attention between her laptop and her planner. "Basically, I was. Being bombarded that intense so instantaneous is shocking, but I never felt unworthy of being with my husband. I know I'm that girl."

"Okay." Mel laughed, snapping her fingers.

"I know that's right, bestie."

"Block out the world's opinions. Focus on keeping your relationship healthy because meshing y'all's beliefs and attitudes takes work, so imagine shouldering everybody else's opinions along with it."

Mel passed Sherrie a sausage, egg, and cheese croissant. I took a big bite out of my vegan breakfast wrap.

This was our tradition. Get together once a week before the shop opens to have a gabfest while eating a great breakfast in Sherrie's office.

Daintily wiping her mouth, Mel inserted her own advice. "Listen, I somewhat understand. Talik is a celebrity of sorts. In the church world, women love pastors and have no shame pursuing a man of God. He and I make sure we're good because our first ministry begins at home. If we can't take care of home, we won't be as effective outside of the home."

Sherrie smiled dreamily. "Mel is absolutely correct. Owen does not play about me."

"He sure doesn't," I said with an amused smirk. They all laughed, knowing exactly what I was alluding to.

Because Owen most certainly did not play about his queen. A few months ago, a guy made a pass at her and wouldn't let up. Owen handed that guy his behind so bad that Otis and Talik had to pull him off the guy.

I'd never seen Owen that mad before.

We all learned first-hand that Owen did not play about Sherrie.

"Victor is so different from what I imagined," I confessed. I felt my mouth curling up into a smile at thoughts of him and how endearing he was.

"What do you mean?" Sherrie asked, gathering her trash.

I pushed my food away. "He's an amazing man. I say that honestly, not because I'm in love with him, but because he's really a good guy. Of course, he's fine."

"And is," Gretchen expressed. Mel and Sherrie agreed.

"He's so intentional and open. That man shares his heart so openly with me. From things he feels are his weaknesses to his failures and his fears. He feels safe with me, and I never want to become unsafe for him." His face when he thought I was breaking up with him after the airport incident still bothered me. Shay gave up on him, and I refused to be another woman to mishandle him. "I feel safe with him too. Maybe this is naïve of me, but I know he'll never betray me. I've never been so sure of someone in my life."

Sherrie held up her hand. "Believe me, we all can see he's deeply in love with you. Y'all's love is so tangible. As soon as y'all walked into the backyard the other day, we all felt it. Even the guys were talking about it."

"Are you serious?"

"Yes," Mel and Gretchen said at the same time.

"I for sure thought maybe y'all were moving too fast because he was freshly divorced, and you and Marty had just broken up. I was mistaken because you and Victor are the real deal."

Confirmation from my girls warmed my heart.

Now, I was waiting on God. I'd asked Him if Victor was the one for me more than once. I'd never felt anything but peace since he and I began our relationship.

Tonight, I'd ask Him again.

Cause I really wanted to marry Victor.

***

I asked God for a sign this morning to show me if Victor was my forever or not. I *really* hoped it was the former.

I needed a hike before work so I could have more one-on-one time with my Lord and Savior.

All through my hike, the sparse hairs on my arms stood at attention. I could feel Victor so strongly this morning. I found myself looking around, but nope, I was alone, save for a few hikers I passed on the trail.

Shaking it off, I prayed and climbed.

But the more I climbed, the more the feelings of awareness intensified.

As I trudged up the hill to my favorite look-out spot, I spied a figure in the distance. Whoever it was sat on the lone bench under the canopy of trees.

Goosebumps peppered my skin.

Lord, am I having a health episode?

Shaking off the irrational thought, I continued to pray.

Anyway Lord, I need your confirmation about your son, and I thank you in advance for said confirmation about your son. I don't want to go any further in a relationship with him if he's not for me. It would break my heart to have to break up and move on because he's been so good to me and I love him so much, but I'll be obedient. It'll definitely be hard, Lord, so I would need your help to move on, but Lord, I pray it's in your will that Victor and I are meant to be. Lord, it would be so hard though, like really excruciating. I know I keep repeating this part because I really don't want to let him go if you say I must, so I sincerely pray you give me a sign that won't leave room for doubt. What am I saying? I mean, you are not the author of confusion, so I know you'll do right by me. It's just I don't want to let him go, Lord. But like I said, I will if I must, and...

I looked up and the face of the person sitting on the bench became clearer.

I stumbled but quickly righted my footing.

Heart pounding and face split into a big grin, I grew a little misty. Hand to chest, I thanked God for confirmation.

So, I was tripping for nothing. You know how I can get. Thank you for always having my best interests at heart. Help me, help us to be good stewards over this relationship. Every day of our forever, keep us, guide us, remind us, and bless us. Amen.

Stopping in front of my forever love, I realized God had given me confirmation as soon as I started my hike. I felt Victor ever since I parked my car.

"I see your knees didn't fail you this morning."

He laughed, and I admired how handsome he looked in this athletic wear. His skin was glistening, and teeth were gleaming in the sunlight.

"I guess this means you're not mad at me anymore."

I quickly shook my head. "I was never mad at you. I was agitated with Tinashay. For her to show up like that, acting crazier than a road lizard. I wanted to put my hands on her. I imagined wrapping my hands around her throat and squeezing until I got ready to let go. That's why I told you I needed a minute."

Understanding dawned on his face. "Oh."

"Yes," I teased. "I said give me a minute, not leave me alone. You left me alone for a full twenty-four hours. What's wrong with you, man?"

Chuckling, he reached for me, and I automatically slid into his arms. Placing a kiss on my sweaty forehead, he mumbled, "I missed you."

I took a sniffed his chest and sighed, feeling right at home.

"I missed you too." So much.

Ch. 15

Victor

My mind, body, and spirit were at peace.

I got the grand idea to wait for Athena at the top of her favorite hiking trail. I'd rehearsed my "baby please" apology on the drive over. I asked God for His assist because every scenario I pictured in my mind, Athena was scowling at me.

I stayed away for nothing.

My presence here on this cliff was actually twofold. I wanted to apologize, and I wanted to reassure her that Tinashay was not a factor.

Athena had all of me.

"I got an emergency restraining order yesterday." Athena jerked back to peer at me. "She's not to come in one-hundred feet of me or you."

"How did you get a restraining order on my behalf?"

"I have my ways. Just know Shay will not be a continuous problem for us. If she tries anything, the boys in blue will be taking her away."

To show my filly how important and how serious I was about us and how much I'd go to protect her, I took the whole day to make some moves.

First up, I went to the courthouse. My celebrity helped me see a judge at the last minute. I gave the judge a quick rundown of Shay's antics, and he signed off on an emergency protective order.

Second, O and I took a short flight to New York.

Third, I called in the big guns. I booked a jet for my family to come to town to meet my girl in person. I also called Ms. Chelsea. She asked for my mom's number so she and my mom could coordinate a family dinner. I received a text last night from my mom gushing over Ms. Chelsea and talking about how excited she was to visit.

Fourth, I called Marianna so she could draft a press release to hit the media the day after the family dinner.

And fifth, I went to O's last night to talk to Gretchen. Before I could say anything, she told me she talked to Ms. Chelsea and my mom earlier. The family dinner was scheduled to be held tomorrow evening in my backyard. All I had to do was leave everything up to the women and show up with Athena at the proposed time.

"We need to talk." I led her to the bench under the trees.

"Sounds ominous," she quipped, settling onto my lap.

I kissed and nuzzled her scented neck. "It's not, trust me. I came up here ready to apologize and to reassure you."

"Reassure me about what?"

"Shay."

Brows furrowed, she asked with an attitude, "Reassure me about *Shay*?"

"Stop frowning." I rubbed her forehead. "Shay is not a threat to us, nor to you."

"Why does everybody keep saying that? I'm not worried at *all* because you're mine. No other woman is a threat to our relationship unless you allow them to be a threat. Now, if you show me with your actions that your attention is elsewhere, you won't have to say a word. I'll chuck up the deuces and keep it moving. I know in the looks department that Shay and I are vastly different, but I know I look good. You know I look good, and I also know that you ain't going anywhere."

I grinned, feeling validated my darn self by my filly's confidence. I told her, "Well, shut it down then."

She laughed, grabbing me around my throat and cupping the back of my head, forcing my head to tilt back.

"Next time, I say I need a minute, I mean give me an hour or two, then you come find me," Athena threatened and bit my bottom lip.

"How about— OW!" I laughed when she nipped my lip harder.

"Don't talk back."

"I ain't Martian."

"His name is Marty and *thank God* because I probably would've ended up having to beat him up."

"I don't know, Filly. His mama looks like one tough cookie. She might KO you to avenge her Martian." We laughed together.

"I got anger on my side, so I'd give her a run for her money."

"If I was a betting man, my money would be on her— OW!"

I think she drew blood that time.

***

"Dang, that thang cutting up in the sunlight," my brother said, admiring the rock Otis helped me pick out for Athena the other day.

"It's very nice." Owen agreed, taking his turn to look the ring over.

Dad leaned closer, "Oh, she's going to love that."

Us guys were huddled around the barbeque grill while the women sat several yards away by the pool. Faith was the only one missing. She was too far along to fly. Mason was going to leave in the morning to get back since they anticipated Baby Cole to show up any day now.

The distance between our groups provided cover so I could show the ring to the guys.

"Congratulations, son. Your mother and I are so proud of you, and I thank God almighty that you found love again." My dad clapped me on the back.

"Thanks, Dad."

O looked at my Dad. "Mr. Will, ya' boy here was trying to get married before his divorce finalized. I had to talk him down."

Talik shocked me by joining in on the ribbing—no, the lying. "Yeah, his nose is an open freeway. The night of the comedy show, he asked us to check his fit and his breath because Athena was coming to the show."

"Sis had him stuttering on stage and everything," Owen added.

I laughed. These lying negroes.

"Dang, bro!" Mason shook his head as if embarrassed.

"How y'all gonna lie on me like that? Pastor, I'm shocked by you the most."

They roared with laughter.

"Son, don't worry about them. They're just busting your chops, but if you need a few pointers on swag, I got you."

"Really Dad?" I shook my head while they all laughed at me.

"I couldn't help myself."

Owen asked, "When are you going to propose?"

"Today."

I was waiting for Gretchen's father to arrive. Athena told me how important he was to her, so being that he was her father figure, I made the drive to Jackson and introduced myself. He gave me his blessing after we had the most intense talk. A talk that left a good impression on me.

Randall Bennett was a reasonable and wise man, but he also did not play about his girls.

Before I left his house, I'd become his son as well.

"Are you nervous, bro?"

"Nervous? Never. Sure? Forever."

O clowned, "My boy got bars. Give 'em the pose, Vic."

I dusted my shoulder off, straightened my shirt, thumbed my nose and clasped my hands down in front of me.

They were so loud, drawing the attention of the women.

I locked eyes with my filly and winked. She blushed and looked away.

I chuckled to myself.

I'm busting' up all that modesty later on.

***

Projector & jumbo inflated screen set up.

Check.

All the guests settled.

Check.

Ring in my pocket.

Check.

Filly sitting to my left.

Check.

Ready to press play.

Click...click....

I hit the remote on the side of my chair.

"What's wrong?" Athena asked.

"The remote's not working."

"Check to see if the batteries are in there."

Right...the batteries. I forgot to put the batteries in. I smiled sheepishly and quickly made my way into the house to find the batteries.

Batteries found in a kitchen drawer, I quickly inserted the batteries and rushed back outside.

"My bad y'all. I forgot to put the batteries in."

Ms. Chelsea leaned forward. "That's alright baby. We're on your time."

I started to sit, then I thought about it. I forgot to do my speech and "fake" explain what this was all about.

"Before I press play, I wanted to explain to y'all that this is not just a movie. Animation is a new thing for me, and it's a pet project that I started working on a few weeks ago. So, what I'm about to show you is a short snippet of what's been completed so far."

"Wow, Victor," Athena gushed. "You didn't tell me you were producing an animated movie. Congratulations!"

"Thank you, baby," I said, retaking my seat. I pulled her seat closer and kissed her neck.

She wiggled in her seat. "Press play. I'm excited."

She just didn't know.

I pressed play, and the movie began.

"Once upon a time, there was a comedic genius named, Victor Cole. He made everyone laugh yet he was a sad man because he'd had his heart broken. Vowing to never love again, Victor made the decision to forever be alone. God looked down and saw how sad Victor was and said to Himself, 'I will heal my son and make him happy again. My son shall not be alone, so I will send Him one of my daughters.' Not long after, Victor was invited to a party. He was having another sad day until he looked up and saw the most beautiful woman in the world. His heart started to thump a little harder as he watched her. At that moment Victor knew he'd found the one. It was during this party, he learned the beauty's name was Athena Rose. Still, he kept his distance because he knew he had to find the broken pieces of his heart and put them back together.

But bad news awaited Victor. He learned Athena had a beau named Martian, who had a dragon for a mother."

Everybody cracked up. Athena, with crying eyes stuck to the screen, laughed behind the hand covering her mouth.

"Victor also knew Martian was a slight inconvenience, and he left the party with a pep in his step, vowing that he'd make Athena his wife one day. One year later, Athena and Victor reunited. At first, Athena played hard to get until Victor's good looks and charm won her heart. Their love developed quickly. Like the nursey rhyme says, 'First comes love, then comes marriage...' So, Athena Nakoma Rose, what do you say?"

The animated characters on screen turned as if looking directly into the camera. Tears streamed down Athena's face. Our people were making a big ruckus all around us, but my focus was on her.

Down on one knee, I pulled her hand away from her mouth and asked, "Athena, I love you and can't imagine life without you. This may seem rushed, but this can't happen fast enough for me. Will you marry me?"

She jerkily nodded before launching into my arms.

Ch. 16

Athena

The movie, the proposal, the love.

The man.

This feeling right now was overwhelming in a good way and everything I could have imagined.

And I couldn't stop crying.

I swiped another tear errant tear while taking another long, admiring look at my ring. The ring...*oh my gosh*...was so beautiful.

The man sitting next to me was beautiful.

Mind, body and spirit.

Loving him took me by surprise. I previously said I wouldn't mind falling like Owen and Sherrie and also like my sis and Otis, but I had no idea the emotions I'd feel or how the whirlwind of a short relationship followed by exchanging vows would overtake me. I figured with Marty that I was fine waiting. I for real was fine with waiting. I just never imagined Marty breaking up with me and the almost immediate start of Victor and me. I never imagined loving Victor this soon and being okay with us going this fast. But now that this moment happened so soon after we started dating, my head was spinning.

Everything was happening so fast.

Though I felt overwhelmed, I couldn't stop the ride.

Wouldn't dare stop the ride.

However, the ride sped up a little bit more because the surprises didn't stop after the proposal.

Victor restarted the movie after everyone calmed down. By the time the credits rolled, I was bawling like a baby.

Victor revealed he'd invested in my clothing line, and I had a meeting with Braedan Harris next week.

Needing a moment away to recenter myself, I told Victor I needed to use the restroom. Giving me a quick kiss on the lips, I stole away while everyone was occupied.

I stayed in the master bathroom for a while just looking around and realizing that this house was about to be mine. I tried to have a coherent prayer with God, but the prayer was so chopped up and unfocused because I was still reeling from everything. I ended up uttering a simple *Thank you, God*. I checked my face one last time before exiting the bathroom. I felt more centered and ready to rejoin my people.

I stepped out the back door and found mayhem awaiting me.

Victor and Mr. Will were struggling to keep my mama and Ms. Joyce from attacking a woman in a tight dress. A camera crew gleefully captured every moment. Gretchen caught my eye, and she hurried towards me with her hands held up.

"What is going on?" I mumbled to myself.

Angry faces were pointed at the woman.

Ms. Joyce snapped, waving her finger in the woman's face, "How dare you intrude on our family moment! This is not Real Hip-Hop of Housewives or no bullcrap like that. This is real life! My son does NOT want you!"

I would laugh about that line later, but hold up...*what she say about her son?* Gretchen reached for me, but I shook her off. I walked closer because I wanted to see if my suspicions were true.

"Is that any way to talk to your daughter-in-law?" the woman taunted.

I sighed. Suspicions confirmed.

Tinashay.

Again.

"Why are you here?"

Tinashay turned around and grinned. "A-then-ahhhh…is it?"

I rolled my eyes. "You know exactly who I am."

A malevolent gleam filled her eyes. Closing the distance between us, she looked me up and down with a sneer. The camera crew followed dutifully. "I didn't mess up your evening, did I?"

I smiled triumphantly, touching my chin with my left hand—the hand with the ring on it—as if in deep thought. Petty, I know, but necessary.

"No, actually, you're right on time to help us celebrate."

Her beady eyes latched onto the ring on my finger. Hate instantly wiped the smirk off her face. She lunged for me. Gretchen pushed her back, and that set Otis off.

Victor ran towards us.

I was not about to fight Tinashay over my man. She'd be fighting by herself because I refused to act out of character because she regretted divorcing Victor. Nope, I was not about to do this.

Instead of engaging, I turned and walked away.

I heard from behind, "Don't walk away from me!" and "Get her!"

I turned to see what was happening, but a hard tackle from behind propelled me into the pool. The shock of the hit and going underwater dazed me. A pair of hands grabbed me under the armpits and pulled me to the surface. Coughing and sputtering, I looked into Victor's eyes.

"I got you," he reassured me.

"She pushed me in the pool!" I snatched away from Victor, looking to see where Tinashay was. If a fight is what she wanted, a fight she was going to get.

I quickly pulled myself out of the pool.

"Athena! Wait, baby. Talik got her, and the police are on the way."

Sopping wet and madder than a den of aggravated rattlesnakes, I stomped past everyone into the house, a trail of water following me back upstairs. I locked myself in the master bath and removed my clothes.

"Lord, I want to get her," I said, walking back and forth across the bathroom floor.

A knock at the door drew my ire.

"Go away!"

"It's me, Filly. Open the door."

Ch. 17

Victor

"It's me, Filly. Open the door." Water dripped from my body onto the floor.

"I'm naked."

"Let me see...uh...I didn't mean to say that."

"Yes, you did, pervert!"

I laughed before I knew it.

I leaned my head against the door. Now was not the time for jokes, but Athena always brought out the kid in me. I loved that about her.

"And stop laughing! Pass me a shirt and a pair of your shorts."

I did as told and knocked on the door again. The door opened a sliver, and her hand eased out. I passed the clothes, and she slammed the door in my face.

"I'm going to change my clothes too, okay?" I waited for an answer. "Athena, you heard me."

"Okay."

Stubborn thing.

In all honesty, she had the right to be mad. I was furious too because Shay had officially lost ALL her marbles by showing up with a film crew. She knew she had a restraining order against her, and I thought after I hadn't heard from her for a few days that she was conceding her campaign against me. In fact, she was plotting. Something I should've anticipated.

My mom was mad.

Ms. Chelsea was mad.

Gretchen, Mel, and Sherrie were mad.

The men were annoyed on my behalf, but they were handling it better than the women.

"Bro, the police want to talk to you downstairs," Mason announced from the doorway.

"Thanks man. I'll be done in a minute. I need to change my clothes."

"Okay." He hesitated for a second. "Is Athena good?"

"She's upset, but I'm going to make it up to her." He nodded and left.

Quickly changing my clothes, I grabbed my phone, grateful it was waterproof. The bathroom door opened, and Athena emerged dressed in my clothes. I bit back a satisfied grin at the vision of her swimming in my clothes.

Pointing at her hair, she said, "Look at my hair." Her hair was a clumpy mess. I could see the separation between the tracks and her leave-out.

I crowded her, pulling her into my arms. "Aww, Filly, it's okay, baby. I promise I'll buy you some more."

Her lips quirked. "Stop trying to make me laugh."

"I'm so sorry Shay ruined our engagement. I promise I did not foresee her showing up with cameras to pledge her undying love and devotion. It's so crazy. It's like I watched the whole thing unfold from outside of my body." I couldn't get over Shay actually doing this to me again, and she messed with my baby. I couldn't let this go.

Athena's face softened. "Our engagement is not ruined. I'm more upset about my hair. I just got it done." Touching my chest, she looked up at me. "You're making jokes, but I feel you. You're upset."

I was furious and trying my best to not let it show.

"I'm tired of keeping quiet while Tinashay is doing all this stupid stuff for attention. I can't take it anymore. Tonight was special for us, and she showed her behind for whatever reason she's conjured up in that sick mind of hers. Just thinking about everything she's said and done to me since we separated got me ready to tell the whole world the truth. But for her to contaminate one of the happiest days of my life is..." My nose flared as I looked away, and I struggled not to lose control.

"Hey, look at me. Give me your eyes, Victor," Athena commanded, touching my face. I took a deep breath to ease the tension in my body before giving her my eyes. "Think about this. Tonight was her breaking point. I want you to genuinely think about it. Her antics didn't change anything tonight. We're still engaged. Our family and friends are still here supporting us. We're still in love. She changed nothing for us. For herself, she's created a set of problems that involves handcuffs and a meeting in front of a judge. Whoever is in charge of the film crew that was here will spill the tea if they haven't already. And everyone will finally see Tinashay for who she is."

I thought about it. Athena was right. "You're right."

"I know." She kissed my lips. "Let's go give our statement to the police."

Walking out hand in hand, I told her, "That tackle was clean though."

She glared at me. "Too...soon."

"I'm sorry."

Seconds later.

"I love you, Victor."

"Love you too, Filly."

***

Ping. Ping. Ping. Ping. Ping. Ping.

"And so it begins," Athena acknowledged, looking down at my phone.

Everyone went home a few hours ago, and my parents and Mason retired upstairs. Athena and I stayed up to cuddle on the sofa and watch old episodes of *Martin*.

Keying in my code (her birthdate), I clicked on the first notification. The headline loomed from the phone: *TINASHAY COLE ARRESTED FOR ASSAULT IN MISSISSIPPI*

"I'm surprised it took this long." I powered off my phone and tossed it on the cushion beside me.

"I'm glad you've calmed down," she said with a lazy drawl. I loved her country twang.

"Yeah."

Yawning, she asked, "What did you do? Run off to the bathroom and crochet a king-size comforter set when we weren't looking?" She barely got the words out because she was laughing so hard.

"Oh, okay. Earlier, I had some compassion for you."

"But you told the joke before you decided to have compassion!"

"Alright, alright. We're even. I got my joke in, and you got your joke in."

"We're even."

We watched tv a moment before…

"Can I see the comforter set?" Giggling, she attempted to get up, but I snatched her behind back down.

I flipped onto her back, pinning her in place. "Take this beating like a woman."

Her carefree laughter was like sweet music to my ears.

What a way to end what could've been a disastrous night.

Ch. 18

Athena

Victor asked me what was the one thing he could do to make up for the whole Tinashay crashing our engagement moment.

I told him, "Nothing."

Because he didn't have to make up anything to me because of her behavior. However, I suspected he needed a do-over of sorts to help him get past yet another ugly scene courtesy of his ex-wife. I sensed his unrest with it because everything he confided in me about his failed marriage unveiled the depth of his hurt and pain. My man was still healing, but Tinashay's continuous provocation and taunting after breaking his heart triggered him every time she went public. He fought through it each and every time. God graced him to maintain his sanity through the ridicule.

So, that's why I asked him what I could do to make things better for him.

He requested a return to St. Lucia.

I immediately went and packed my bags.

We were on day three of our impromptu getaway. And yes, we informed our people this time around.

I don't know how he managed it, but Victor re-booked the two-bedroom villa the same as last time. The ocean view was still gorgeous.

Standing at the railing of the balcony, I closed my eyes and let peace wash over me. Arms snaked around my waist, and I allowed my body to mold to his.

"What are you thinking about out here?" Linking our left hands, he lifted them up. Our wedding bands sparkled in the sunlight.

"Everything. I can't believe we got married." Literally an hour ago in our swimsuits at a resort chapel.

I escaped to the balcony to process the monumental decision we just made. Don't get me wrong, I regretted nothing, but I needed time to...process.

Victor turned me around, a question in his eyes I directly answered.

"I love you, and I'm happy we did this."

Awareness surged between us.

No other words were needed. My husband picked me up in his arms and carried me into our suite until we reached the bedroom. Roses and sunflowers sprinkled over the covers, and flutes of champagne sat on a tray near the foot of the bed.

Wordlessly, Victor deposited me on the bed, briefly leaving me to remove the tray. He rejoined me on the bed. Making light work of removing our swimwear and our bodies touching, Victor hovered over me gazing down at me with a tender expression. I shivered at the light stroke of his finger down my face. His lips replaced his finger, following the same path.

The second strongest strand eternally tethered us together.

***

Totally languid, we lay on our sides staring into one another's eyes.

"What we just did..." I began.

"Yeah..." He yawned like a contented king of the jungle.

"I think I'm pregnant with twins."

He roared with laughter.

***

Victor finished setting up the laptop. He patted his lap, and I eased down.

"Why are you so anxious?" he probed.

I was surprised he picked up on it. Feeling him was more my superpower. I thought I hid my surprise, but he smiled at me knowingly.

"You feel me, and I feel you because our souls became one yesterday. Talk to me, Filly."

"My mama might get angry. I promised her years ago I would never elope and that I'd plan a proper wedding with her."

"She may surprise you."

I shook my head. "You don't know Chelsea Rose."

"Give her a chance, but if she gets upset, I have your back. We'll navigate angry mama waters together, okay?"

"Okay." His support helped me relax.

A few minutes later, our loved ones' and friends' faces filled the screen. My mama was smiling from ear to ear. I took that as a good sign.

"What's up people?" Victor greeted.

Everyone called out their greetings.

Gretchen squinted at us then blurted, "Looks like y'all played hide the pickle and enjoyed it."

I covered my mouth to hide my cheshire grin as different octaves of "What!" and "Hide the pickle?" flowed through the laptop's speakers.

"Well, Gretchen," Victor answered with a smirk, "in the words of Lionel Richie...*all night long*."

Oh my God! He really said that in front of our parents.

Mouths dropped, and shock filled faces. Then, they started overtalking one another.

I heard Otis singing the chorus to the song.

Victor muted them. "Hold up, y'all. One at a time."

"Is hiding a pickle a euphemism for sex?" Ms. Joyce asked first, sounding confused. Everyone busted out laughing.

"Yeah, Mom," Mason responded through laughter.

I chanced a peep at my Mama. Her face was stern.

Through clenched teeth, I expressed to Victor, "Clear the air, please."

"Right, right. We did not have premarital sex. We eloped!"

My mama's face crumbled.

Oh no. I felt horrible. Batting back my own tears, I rushed to apologize.

"Mama, I'm sorry I broke my promise. Please don't cry."

Everyone looked at the screen concerned.

Shaking her head, she wiped her tears. "No, baby. I'm not upset at all. I'm happy for you and Victor. All I ever wanted was for you to meet and marry the man God had for you. You did, and I couldn't be happier."

Relieved, I whispered a trembly, "Thank you, Ma."

Victor kissed my temple. "I told you." He did.

"Congratulations, son and daughter," Daddy Randall chimed in.

"Yes, congratulations. I'm so proud of you, Victor. I can't wait to get to know you more, Athena," Mr. Will said, rubbing his weeping wife's shoulders.

"I can't wait to get to know you and Ms. Joyce more as well."

"Mom, you good?" Victor asked.

She shook her head, wiping her tears. "I'm too full right now."

I understood how she felt. Since the proposal, I'd been too full.

"Y'all kept the tradition," Talik said, filling the silence.

"Trying be like us," Otis joked.

Victor laughed. "I had to get like y'all in the Sip."

Mason asked, "What tradition?"

"Marrying fast. I married Sherrie barely a month after we went on a road trip, and Otis drunk married Gretchen in Vegas when we went out there to celebrate Talik and Mel," Owen volunteered.

Mel addressed Mason. "The tradition skipped us, but our whirlwind courtship made up for it."

I did let everyone know that we were going to have a real ceremony sometime in the near future. My girls then informed me that they were going to plan a bridal shower.

"I need help planning, y'all."

Mel grinned. That was right up her alley.

Sherrie said, "You know I got you on the dress."

Mama added, "Count me and Joyce in."

"I have so many ideas," Ms. Joyce boasted.

"May God have mercy on you," Victor whispered in my ear, and I snickered.

Another twenty minutes of laughs, planning, and Faith's update about a scheduled c-section, we ended the Zoom.

I collapsed on the bed. "Whew, I need a nap."

"We both do."

True because yesterday's extracurricular activities spanned into the night and into the wee hours of the morning.

Victor scooped me up, and we slid under the covers.

My eyes grew heavy within seconds.

Ping. Ping. Ping. Ping. Ping. Ping.

We groaned at the same time.

"Turning it off," he said, reaching for his phone. "Whatever it is can wait until tomorrow."

Ch. 19

Victor

Miracles happen every day, and I've witnessed some of the most awe-inspiring miracles happen for people.

Last week, unbeknownst to me, I was next in line for my own miracle.

Deep in the throes of marital bliss, Marianna called me with good news. First, rewind back to the press release that was overshadowed by Shay's arrest. Marianna revamped it and released it again to announce our marriage. I posted a few pictures of our wedding bands (comments got turned off) the day of the press release.

But here's the miracle.

Shay recanted every lie she ever told about me during a LIVE she did once she found out Athena and I actually got married.

Who wouldn't serve a God like this?!

At the beginning of this whole ordeal, God told me to wait it out, just be quiet because He would work everything together for my good, and He did.

She confessed to cheating. She confessed to having an abortion without my knowledge. She confessed to lying about writing my jokes. She confessed to stealing two million dollars from me. That was news to me. She apologized to her friends and followers for lying and told how getting arrested helped her see the light. She ended the video by saying she was going away to seek healing etc.

Social media was shook!

And the same ones who slandered my name were the same ones who turned on Shay. She had to delete her IG account. But snippets of her video confession were still circulating social media and entertainment news outlets.

God lifted the gag order too.

I made the decision, if the opportunity presented itself, that I would vaguely answer questions about Shay.

The opportunity came sooner than I anticipated.

***

"If you're just tuning in, welcome to another live episode of Black Bros. Comedy Podcast. I'm your host, W. L. Martin, and alongside me is my co-host, Rob 'The Heartthrob' McIntire. We got the G.O.A.T.

here in the studio. That's right folks, Victor Cole is here. Before the commercial break, you talked about your upcoming retirement show. I still can't believe you're hanging up the mic, Vic."

I laughed. "I know, but when you know it's time to hang it up, it's time to hang it up."

Rob added, "But you're leaving on a good note. You and Otis Davis did the Netflix special last year, and it killed. I'm going to say it's one of the best shows I've ever seen."

"I appreciate that. I'm proud of it, and O is proud of it too. I handpicked every known and unknown comic that did the show."

"Let's talk about the unknown comics. They were quality dudes who owned the stage like seasoned vets."

I nodded. "Yeah, they did. That's exactly why I chose them because they know the art of comedy. It's not a popularity contest for them. It's all about the love of comedy for them and knowing how to create symmetry between the setting up of the joke to the actual punchline. They were hungry, and I knew they were a good fit for the show. And they also write their own material. It's different performing someone else's material versus performing what you created yourself."

W.L. commented, "Right, I'm more hype to perform what I write for the audience. It definitely hits different."

Rob backed him up. "No doubt."

"You are winning from the stage to entrepreneurship to now as a husband again. Congratulations on your marriage. I saw you wife, and she's gorgeous."

I grinned. "Thanks man, Athena is definitely gorgeous inside and out."

Rob threw out, "Can't say the same about the first one."

W.L. chuckled, and I shook my head.

"Maybe I'm being too harsh, but Vic, man…you went through some ish with your ex. I'ma say it with my chest live so everybody listening can hear when I say you are a strong man to go through what you did for a year in silence. Brotha, I don't know how you didn't retaliate."

"Very strong. The divorce was public, and people added fuel to the fire every time a new story dropped. How did you navigate the separation, the allegations, and then the subsequent divorce?"

I cleared my throat. "Honestly, God got me through. For over a year, I remained silent because God told me to keep my mouth shut. He said He'd fight my battle. I won't lie to you nor W.L. It was one of the hardest things I had to do. So yeah, I prayed a lot and worked on my heart. I refused to grow bitter."

Rob added, "For a year, three-hundred and sixty-five days, you stayed in the blogs most of those days. Before we could get over one headline, another dropped. The allegations got more outrageous I feel because you didn't respond. The one that got me was about Tinashay writing your jokes. Anyone in the comedy world knows you write your own stuff."

"I do."

W.L. pointed out, "People took your silence as an admission of guilt when your silence was really you being the bigger person. The think pieces written and the added fuel to the already raging gender war between Black men and Black women also influenced people's opinions about your perceived guilt."

"So, here's the thing. I've had dudes walk up to me bashing my ex and Black women in general, and I immediately stopped them in their tracks. No matter what my ex did to me, I refuse to degrade her. As for Black women, I love y'all. I will not engage in bashing our women because I've been hurt by one and refuse to get the help I need to heal and move on. Black men need Black women, and Black women need Black men. The gender war would stop when we collectively realize that this is not about gender, it's about human behavior. Assign the behavior to the person and not the gender. When my ex did what she did, I didn't say all Black women are trash. I would never because I know some amazing Black women. I come from an amazing Black woman. My sister-in-law is an amazing Black woman. I have aunts, cousins, and friends who are phenomenal Black women. My wife Athena is a Black woman who I love and thank God for every day. That Black woman came into my life and changed me for the better. After a couple months of dating, I asked her to marry me. A few days later, we were married. At the end of the day, I refuse to reject our women because that would be like rejecting myself."

W.L. nodded his vigorously. "Facts."

"I love my Black queen too. Final question, W.L."

"My question is after everything, have you forgiven Tinashay?"

"I have. That wasn't easy either because I'm human. My name was trashed, and some of my business deals were on shaky ground. I am grateful she did the LIVE video. It vindicated me, and I pray she gets the healing she deserves. I wish her the best."

Rob joked, "That's a good man, Savannah."

W.L. and I laughed.

***

"Victor, baby, you were so good and poised the entire interview. I'm so proud of you for not going in on Tinashay. You've been very graceful. I think it's one of the sexiest attributes you have."

I swooped her up into my arms. "Sexiest attribute?"

She grinned. "One of the sexiest attributes."

I checked the time on my watch. "It's time to go. Marianna is waiting for us at her office."

"Lead the way, mister."

I escorted my beautiful, Black woman out to the truck where JB was waiting to take us to my meeting with Marianna.

"How you liking Cali so far, Athena?" JB asked, changing lanes.

When they met the other day, she told him she'd never been to Los Angeles. They totally ignored me and conversed all the way from the airport to my parent's house. I watched their interaction, glad they hit it off. JB instantly liked Athena. He later told me that he could tell she was genuine and the right one for me by the way she catered to me and openly showed her affection. Said he'd never seen all my teeth before. He also said Shay was the total opposite. I'd never thought about it, but he was right. Shay didn't like public displays of affection, and she always preferred that I do all the catering to her. I gave a lot, and it was never appreciated.

Athena leaned forward. "I'm loving it. It's not Copeland, but so far, I'm having a good time. We've hit some of the spots I've always wanted to visit, and tomorrow, Victor is taking me to Venice Beach."

"Make him to take you shopping on Rodeo Drive." JB winked at her in the rearview window.

Athena turned to me with a teasing grin. "Black Ninja, I'm going to need use your black card."

JB laughed, and I smirked at her. "Whatever you want, Mrs. Cole."

A funny look passed over her face.

"What's up?" I asked her, wondering what she was thinking.

"I keep forgetting my last name is different."

Pulling her closer to me, I whispered in her ear, "I'll help you remember later on."

"Stop being mannish." She blushed, snuggling closer to me. "So, JB are you ready to uproot your life and move to Mississippi?"

He shook his head, shooting her a playful glare. "You're just as bad as Vic. I'm still thinking over my answer."

I offered him the opportunity to move to Copeland, and I'd help him start his own driving service. He asked for a couple days to think it over, but Athena and I gave him a nudge in our own way.

"Oh, please, you know you're coming to Copeland. I don't know why you're playing hard to get."

He laughed. "Maybe I'm moving, maybe I'm not."

"You are moving," Athena countered, and I laughed.

Her phone chimed, alerting her to a Duo Call coming through. She looked at the phone and squealed.

"My babies!" she grinned from ear to ear at Sherrie and Gretchen holding their baby girls.

I couldn't wait to put a grin on her face about our children.

I planned to work on that soon.

Ch. 20

Athena

"Marty, what are you doing here?" I crossed my arms, blocking his view into Victor and I's home.

In a pair of creased khakis and with a repentant look on his face, he issued a contrite, "Can we talk?"

Tapping my chin thoughtfully, I said, "I'm trying to decide whether it's because you look so much like your mama or because you're wearing starched khakis, which I'm sure she pressed, that's making me mad. I'm going to go with both."

"Athena—"

Palm up in his face, I shook my head. "No, don't even. You have some nerve to come to my home disrupting a romantic evening with my husband for whatever this foolishness is. Marty, you broke up with me, then proceeded to further humiliate me by disparaging me to the tabloids and blogs because you felt I should've been pining after you. Chile, the comedy. I wish I would pine behind a man whose mother has to still cut up his meat, so he won't choke. You wasted my time, and—"

What was I doing? My anger was probably sending the wrong message, so I switched gears. "How about this? I forgive you, and I also need to thank you."

Marty asked, confused, "Thank me for what?"

I smiled. "For vacating my life so my husband could fill that spot. So, thank you for showing me what I didn't deserve because I learned through Victor what I did deserve. That man came in intentional and put a ring on my finger after two months of dating. I got my forever love because you saw we were not meant to be."

His face fell. "I'm sorry I listened to Mother, and I'm sorry for fueling the lies about you to the media. I was mad because Mother convinced me to break up with you. To her, you weren't good enough. I think any woman I bring around won't be good enough. For what it's worth, I did care about you a lot, and I'm sorry for not allowing us the time to really see where our relationship would go."

I arched an eyebrow. "Nowhere. The relationship was going nowhere, so please absolve yourself."

"Are you really happy with him?" Hope in his eyes shined back at me. And I *hoped* he did not think he still had a chance.

His hopeful look expanded.

Sigh.

Guess I had to be a hope killer today.

"Can I ask you something?"

Eager, he stepped closer. "Sure. You can ask me anything."

Where was this eagerness before, Marty? He was textbook case of men not appreciating a woman until she was gone, and they wanted to spin the block once they realized she was a good woman.

No spinning today.

Not with me.

Not ever.

I shifted on my feet and leaned against the door jamb. "You know how you pray and ask God for something. Then, for years that something eludes you. You continue to believe, and then because you want it so bad, you believe something that fits the description is God answering your prayer. After some time, that something is revealed as a counterfeit, right?"

Marty nodded, probably wondering where I was going with this.

"The counterfeit worked for so long because it looked like it fit the desires of your heart. However, your heart never quite felt fulfilled. Even though you have what you think is God's blessing, true fulfillment eludes you. So, you start convincing yourself that maybe if you stick it out and try that maybe, just maybe you can grow to love it. Truthfully, you end up settling for something that isn't God's best for you. Are you following me?"

"I am." I could see he was following, but he still hadn't grasped the message.

"As I was saying, you settled for something that's not God's best. Then that something starts to disintegrate, and you double down, trying to hold onto it while knowing God is allowing it to break down. Until..." I shake my head, "that something does what you can't do. It does what it was supposed to do. The forced connection between you and it is severed. Do you know what happens next? When your defenses are down and your expectations are shaken up, God sends what He's had for you all along. It doesn't look the way you expected it to look. It doesn't walk and talk the way you expect it to walk and talk. It's...different, but it's everything, *everything* you ever desired. And you realize God always knew best, and you could have avoided the previous disappointment if you had just waited on Him."

I beckoned Marty closer, and he inched closer, ready to hear my next words.

"To answer your question, Marty. I've never been happier because I finally have God's best."

His countenance fell as clarity finally occurred.

"I'm not trying to be mean, but I am being honest with you. I pray God's best finds you too, Marty."

Marty stood still as a statue, rapidly blinking. *Dear God, I hope he doesn't cry.* As if coming out of a trance, he nodded and backed away.

"Well, I'm happy for you, Athena."

"Thanks."

He turned and slowly walked away.

"Marty?"

He halted and turned around. "Yeah?"

"Leave your mother out of your next relationship."

He bobbed his head up and down and trekked back to his car.

I slowly closed the door and turned to find Victor standing behind me with a relaxed look on his face. "The Martian has returned to Mars."

I laughed, easing into his arms. "Have some compassion. His feelings are hurt right now."

"I have no compassion for a man who wants my wife. He better be glad I didn't open the door."

"Simmer down, Black Ninja." I tugged his beard and stood on my toes to kiss his lips.

He palmed my butt and dropped another kiss on my lips.

"Come eat. I finished dinner while you were entertaining your extraterrestrial."

I laughed, following him to the kitchen.

The table was nicely set with lit candles and a vase of roses and sunflowers. Reminded me of our first date.

"Here's your plate." Victor ceremoniously sat a steaming plate of smothered green beans and rice down in front of me.

"Thank you, sir."

He joined me moments later with his plate and quickly blessed the food. Our dinner was lively since we were celebrating our one-month anniversary. We talked about his upcoming events, and I gushed again over the meeting I had with Braedan Harris when we were in L.A. the other week. California was such a time. I was able to get to know my in-laws better. I met my new niece. Faith had a beautiful baby girl who she named Cherish. We were also able to attend church for the first time as a couple.

Pushing my plate away, I asked, "What's for dessert?"

He wiggled his eyebrows and produced a can of whip cream. "Guess," he said, standing and walking out of the kitchen.

I chased him to the bedroom, giggling the entire time.

Later that night, I sat up watching my husband sleep with a contented heart. Victor Cole may not have fit the expectations I held for the one, but he darn sure fit the desires of my heart. I tried hard to hold onto Marty, and I really thought I was right to stay with him, but I've never been happy to be so wrong in my life.

Victor came into my life at the right time, sweeping me off my feet.

He was not my choice, but He was God's choice for me.

I was perfectly okay with that.

Epilogue

Surrounding me on stage were my wife, my family, and my friends. I'd just finished my last set, and the crowd gave me a standing ovation.

"Before I leave the stage," I said to the quieting crowd, "I want to say from the bottom of my heart that I appreciate the love and support you've shown me over the years. I'm blessed to have made it to the top when many didn't get this far. God has been good to me."

"Amen, baby," Mom cosigned along with the crowd.

"Y'all haven't seen the last of me. For now, for the last time, L.A. Y'all've been good." I gave them a two-finger salute.

Whistles and claps filled the room. I walked away from the microphone holding Athena's hand. I was officially retired, and I retired with the right person by my side.

Backstage, I received congratulatory expressions from so many people that their faces became a blur. The photographer Marianna hired gathered up celebrities and other people loitering around for a lengthy photoshoot. Between flashes, I looked for Athena to make sure she was okay. Our eyes would meet, and she'd smile a reassuring smile my way.

An hour later, I finally broke away from everyone to get to my filly.

"Come with me," I whispered in her ear.

I quickly maneuvered us through the lingering crowd of people to the stairwell.

"Want me to carry you?" I looked down at her feet encased in the sky high Loubs I bought her for tonight. They perfectly matched the short, figure-hugging white dress that showed off my filly's legs.

"I can make it."

By the fifteenth flight of stairs, she changed her mind. I stopped for her to hop on my back and climbed the remaining ten flights. She hopped down on the top landing, and I opened the door leading to the roof of the building.

Athena twirled, making the short skirt of her dress flare even more. She smiled at me. "I've never been at the top of a building like this before."

I slipped my hands into my pockets, watching my wife and feeling pleased to offer her another first experience. We'd had several of those since we married a few months ago.

"What made you bring me up here?"

"I needed a minute alone with you."

Her smile grew bigger before she turned back to the view. Easing up behind her, I pulled her close and nuzzled her neck.

"The view is gorgeous."

We enjoyed the view for a while before I spoke again.

"This is how I feel."

Tilting her head back to look at me, she asked, "How do you feel?"

"On top of the world." I was winning at life. In my faith, with my wife, my family, and my career.

"I feel like this every day with you."

This woman knew how to make me feel good. Married life took work, but it didn't have to be hard work with the right person. My filly was beautiful, sexy, spiritually balanced, compassionate, and exactly right for me. Our marriage may have been young, and it was not without a few disagreements, but God strengthened our bond daily.

"Even when I get on your nerves?" I teased her.

She turned and draped her arms around my neck with a big smile. "Even then."

"What about when I interrupt you when you're working?"

She scrunched her nose up. I laughed knowing she hated when I did that.

"Yep."

"When I forget to take the trash out?"

"All the time, Victor. I'm always swept up in you."

I grinned down at her, knowing I was just as swept up in her too.

The End.

Note from Latoya

Hey y'all! I hope you all enjoyed *Swept Up In Him*. Yes, it's a spinoff, but I made it Book 5 of the Blooming Series. I loved writing about Athena & Victor. The idea to write their story came to me not long after Gretchen and Otis's story. I figured I'd make Gretchen's bestie and Victor's second bestie a couple. So, their significant others had to skedaddle. I, myself, did not like Marty for Athena. I knew from the ending of Resurging Big that she would not stay with him because she was settling. Anyway, this series is officially complete (unless another character taps me on the shoulder).

Please, don't be shy. Write me an honest review on Amazon. Reviews make my books visible to new and old readers. I believe what I write is ministry, so you're reviews help spread my ministry to others. Thanks for your continued support. I appreciate each and every one of you. Until next time...

Blessings,

Latoya

Stay up to date on future releases by joining Latoya Garrett's email list at the website below.

Connect with Latoya:

FACEBOOK @authorlatoyagarrett

INSTAGRAM @authorlatoyagarrett

X (TWITTER) @authorlatoyag

YOUTUBE @authorlatoyagarrett

EMAIL: inspirationbytoyadenae@gmail.com

Website: (Books/Updates/Merch)

https://www.authorlatoyagarrett.com

All Links:

https://linktr.ee/toyadenae

Latoya's Catalog

Fiction

The Rosewood Series:

Attitude of Gratitude

To My Surprise

Free to Love

Mending A Bruised Spirit

Two Hearts Plus One

Southern Love Anthology paperback (books 1-4)

Queens In The Making Series:

Sarah: Changing Seasons (Standalone prequel)

Changes I've Made

Leaving My Past Behind

No Holding Back

Blooming Series:

Blooming Big

Loving Big

Resurging Big

Christmas In Copeland

Blooming Spinoff:

Swept Up In Him

Woke Up Series:

I Woke Up Like This

Wake Me, I'm Dreaming

Standalone Titles:

Admired In Secret

Doing Him A Favor

Our Pajamas Matched

Real One

Vanished (Coming 2024)

Non-fiction

The Little Girl In You

In Spite Of It All

My Journey To Pretty

Dear Young Woman Vol. 3

Confident Is She Anthology: A Queen's Guide To Reclaiming Her Throne & Reigning With Conviction

Made in the USA
Columbia, SC
11 November 2024